Never Gonna Be Wifey:

Renaissance Collection

Never Gonna Be Wifey:

Renaissance Collection

Racquel Williams

www.urbanbooks.net

Urban Books, LLC
300 Farmingdale Road, NY-Route 109
Farmingdale, NY 11735

Never Gonna Be Wifey: Renaissance Collection

ISBN 13: 978-1-945855-84-9
ISBN 10: 1-945855-84-3

First Mass Market Printing November 2018
First Trade Paperback Printing June 2018
Printed in the United States of America

10 9 8 7 6 5 4 3 2 1

Distributed by Kensington Publishing Corp.
Submit orders to:
Customer Service
400 Hahn Road
Westminster, MD 21157-4627
Phone: 1-800-733-3000
Fax: 1-800-659-243

Dedication

I dedicate this book to my three sons: Malik, Jehmel, and Zahir. Words can never explain the love I feel for all three of you. I am blessed to be able to be on this journey and to be able to watch y'all grow up. I love you guys with everything in me. I pray Allah continues to bless and protect my greatest treasures.

Acknowledgments

First and foremost, I give all praises to Allah. Without him, none of this would be possible. I am forever grateful and definitely blessed.

To my mom Rosa, thank you for being a rock in my life and also the lives of my boys.

To my other half Carlo, you made it possible for me to focus on being a full-time writer. You are the force behind the scene. Thank you.

To my sister Papaya, blood couldn't make us any closer. Thanks for sticking with me through the laughter and the tears. I love you.

To Stacey Thomas, Ebonee Abbey, Charmaine Galloway, I can't thank you guys enough, but please know I appreciate the love and support. I am forever grateful.

To Ambria Davis, I called you my little sister because you are just that. I am happy that our path crossed, and we are able to weather this storm together.

Acknowledgments

To Rita and Charles King, two of my biggest supporters, I appreciate the love that you guys have shown me.

To Kiera Northington, Smith Sharlene, and Chyta Curry, thank you, ladies, for the long talks and words of encouragement. I appreciate it.

To Tasha Bynum, thanks for the constant promotion of my work. I appreciate you.

To my readers that are always around with words of encouragement and showing me love, no matter what I'm going through, please know I appreciate y'all: Nicki Williams, Rhea Wilson, Qiana Drennen, Barbara Morgan, Dawn Jackson, Cherri Johnson, Mary Bishop, Kendra Littleton, Toni Futrell, Priscilla Murray, Joyce Dickerson, Nola Brooks, Beverly Onfroy, Erica Taylor, Yvonne Covington, Evelyn Johnson, Dessiree Ellison, Donica James, Cherita Price, Nawlinz Robinson, Redgirl Pettrie, Alexis Goodwyn, Mellonie Brown, Tonya Tinsley, Pam Williams, Tammy Rosa, Antinqua Bradby, Venus Murray, Shann Adams, Nancy Pyram, Tina Simmons, Nikki Macnifcent, Kenia Michelle, Jenise Brown, Kysha Small, Suprenia Hutchins, MzNicki Ervin, Trina Mcguire, Rebecca Rogers, Stephanie Wiley, Tera Kinsley-Colman, and Kesia Ashworth-Lawrence.

To the Literary Divas of Spartanburg, ladies, I appreciate the support y'all have given me. I am forever grateful.

Shout out to the Sisters of Essence Book Club, Eva Lee, Sonja Cooks, and the other ladies. I appreciate all the love!

Shout out to all my family in the U.S., Canada, and England, too many to name. I love y'all.

Shout out to my BDP family, thanks for supporting me!

Prologue

"Rock of ages, cleft for me, let me hide myself in thee; Let the water and the blood from thy wounded side which flowed, be of sin the double cure; Save from the wrath and make me pure," the voice of a stocky woman echoed through the loudspeakers.

There was something 'bout that song and the way the words sounded that sent chills up my spine. I couldn't take it; my head was spinning, and my legs trembled as I walked toward the front of the church. I quickly noticed, the church was packed to capacity. I didn't want to be there, not for him, and definitely not with my child. I looked down on my baby. He didn't have a care in the world. He just smiled at me with those bright, big eyes just like his daddy's. I held him closer to my chest and hugged him tight as I tried my best to hold my balance.

The closer I got to the casket, the more my body quaked; I felt clammy, and my heart slammed against my chest. I stood there frozen in place as I stared into the face of the only man that I've ever loved. His face looked unfamiliar. He was swollen and black as midnight. I touched his cold, hard face and rubbed his hair. Tears rolled down my face as I bent down to kiss him on the cheek.

"Alijah, babyyyyyy!" I screamed out in pain. My heart was trying to jump out of my body.

"Grab the child. She's about to fall," a man's voice hollered.

Everything around me turned dark, and the room spun around on its axis. Water gathered in my mouth as my knees gave in, and I fell to the floor.

I woke up minutes later, but I still wasn't feeling good. I looked for my baby. *Where the hell is my child?* I thought.

"Where's my son?" I asked weakly.

"You fainted a few minutes ago. His grandmother has him," some woman said.

I was rushed to Kingston Public Hospital. Man, this hospital was ratchet as hell. People were lying all over the floor, waiting to be seen. A nurse brought me a little wooden stool, and that's where I was at for about three hours.

When I finally got a chance to see the doctors, they did a little bullshit-ass checkup and sent me to a little cube they call a room.

I was happy to be able to relax a little bit, 'cause it was the worst day of my life, and being in this place wasn't helping any. I'd never imagined in a million years that I would be at Alijah's funeral. Life was unfair; we never got a chance to live our lives the way we had intended. We had big plans, to have more babies, but now I can't. I can't wear his last name—nothing. Everything was over for us.

I lay in the hospital bed with tears flowing and replayed all the events that had happened over the past two years. Looking back now, it seemed like we never had a chance from the beginning. *How could life be this cruel?* I thought. All I wanted was to be loved, and the only man that ever gave a fuck about me was taken away without warning.

I felt like I didn't want to live anymore. I was ready to go be with my man. This shit was not fair at all.

"Why, God? You should've let me die." I looked up with tears rolling down my face. I knew I was being selfish, but the pain that I felt was like a sharp knife cutting my heart into tiny pieces, and it was becoming unbearable!

"Hey, honey, how you feeling?" Jeanette asked as she entered the room.

"Feeling? I'm not feelin' much of anything." I shook my head.

"I can't say I understand how you're feeling, but you have to get it together for Azir's sake. He already lost one parent. He deserves to have at least one," she said while she rubbed my back.

I looked at her with tears in my eyes. I never figured out where her strength came from, but even through Alijah's death and me almost being killed, she had been the one that was holding everything down.

"God should've let me die with him. He's my e'erythin'. Since you have answers for e'erythin', why don't you tell me how I'm supposed to go on from here? I lost e'erythin'. You hear me, every fucking thing!" I screamed.

"Sierra, shut the fuck up talkin' like that. I thought I lost you when you was on that floor. I got on my knees in that hospital, and I begged God for mercy. I begged him to save my child's life. I even told him to take my life instead. I know I'm not the most righteous person, but I know God is able to work many miracles; don't you start being ungrateful—you need to be thanking him, 'cause Azir could have been an orphan right now," my mother barked back.

I wasn't in the mood to argue with this self-righteous bitch, so I closed my eyes and let my mind wander off into a fantasy world.

I must have dozed off because I was awakened by the sound of voices arguing. I thought I was trippin' off the narcotics that I had earlier, but soon found out that I wasn't.

"Yo, what the fuck is going on in here?" I yelled.

Jeanette and Alijah's mom turned their attention to me. They seemed surprised.

"Sorry, baby, but Miss Thing here come up in here talking about she want to keep Azir out here in Jamaica. She done lost her goddamn mind."

"What you talking about?" I then turned to his mother for some kind of clarification.

"Sierra, mi cum here in peace. Mi not tryin'a cause nuh trouble. Alijah was mi only pickney, and all mi 'ave left is Azir. All mi asking is to let him stay wit' mi until you get back 'pon yuh foot."

"I'm lost! You're the same woman that called me a home wrecker. The same one that didn't think I was good enough for her son. Now you are here talking 'bout you come in peace. No, there's no fucking peace! Azir is *my* fucking son that I pushed outta *my* pussy. And I will *not* let you or anyone else play Mommy to him. I'm good, and best believe, he's going to be good.

Trust me, I understand you love your son, but you won't use mine to replace him," I spat at her with venom in my voice.

I glanced at her. This was Alijah's mom, the same bitch that cussed me out in the hospital, who talked to me like I wasn't no good for her damn son. Yes, it's her, same old wicked bitch, only this time, she appeared as if she lost a great amount of weight. Her body looked frail, and her eyes were dark; they sank inside of her head as if she lacked days of sleep. In that instant, I felt some kind of pity for her, not because I felt like she deserved it, but because I knew how close she and her son were. I couldn't imagine how I would feel if it was my child. I wouldn't be able to stand here. I would be in a coffin.

"Come here." I motioned for her to come closer to my bed, and she practically fell into my arms. We hugged and cried together. The harder we cried, the tighter we hugged.

"I'm sorry for the way I treated you. I didn't know how Shayna really was. She had me fooled until Alijah told me everything that she did to him. I was shocked and hurt, because I treated her as my own. I do tell you, that boy loved you," she said as she wept.

I don't know why I was hugging this woman. But I know Alijah loved us both, and he would want us to be here for each other. That was enough confirmation for me when I heard her say Alijah loved me. I squeezed her tighter as the tears flowed freely. We finally let go of each other, and I glanced at Jeanette. I sensed a bit of jealousy coming from her.

Jeanette was like a mama pit bull. She was out for blood when it came down to me, even though at times she got on my nerves. I kind of loved the feeling that someone had my back. I knew we had a long way to go, but I knew in due time, we would get there.

"Miss Jeanette, mi sorry fi cum up in here like dis. I kno' yo' love fo' har is strong, and as a madda, mi understand, 'cause I would protect mine if he were still here."

"I understand; it's just that she's been through enough as it is. So when you were saying you wanted her baby, it kind of rubbed me the wrong way. I wasn't the best of anything for her when she was young, but I'm here now, and they gotta kill me first before I let another person hurt her."

My mother was right. I had been through too much shit. Dealing with Shayna's crazy ass and now the death of Alijah. A bitch can't take anymore. Anything else would be a death sentence on my soul. They continued talking, totally ignoring the fact that I was in the room.

"Y'all, I'm right here. And I'm not going any-where," I said. It was getting too hectic in the room.

We continued talking about Shayna and all the wicked shit she has done. His mother was shocked when I broke it down and let her know. I promised her that I would think about leaving Azir with her for a few months. A year at the most while I get myself together. She thanked me and left out.

"Are you sure you want to leave your baby down here? Sierra, you don't really know noth-ing about these people. You know Alijah, not his damn family," Jeanette lashed out.

"To be honest, I think it would be a good move to leave Azir with her, because we will be returning to the States in a few days, and I have no idea what my future will hold."

The feds took my home and the money that was in the safe downstairs. I wasn't sure how deep their investigation was. I need to call my lawyer to find out what's up before I even step foot on that plane.

I'm happy I wasn't a fool and had a little something saved for rainy days. I also knew that Alijah had several accounts in the Cayman Islands and Jamaica, so Azir was set for life. That dude was definitely a street dude, but he was no dumbass nigga. He had his shit well put together when it comes down to his money.

A day later, I was released from the hospital. That IV they gave me definitely gave me an energy boost, along with all Jeanette's pep talk. After I left the hospital, I was a woman on a mission; I needed to visit Alijah's grave. Jeanette tried to convince me that I was in no shape to visit him. I had to; I was his woman and his bottom bitch. He was buried in a cemetery not far from his family home. I totally ignored what she was saying. This was one of the times her ass was getting on my nerves with that all that preaching shit.

I got out of the car and walked toward the graves until I saw the Jackson plot. I promised myself I would not fall out; I had to make it to him. I walked over to his grave and stood there, frozen in place. I rubbed my hand across the cross that his name was written on. I smiled because I knew how much he hated the name "Benjamin." Right about now, Alijah Benjamin Jackson didn't sound bad at all. Matter of fact, I would give up everything to hear him say his full government name out loud. Then fuss about how much he hated that name.

"Baby, I hope you can hear me. I know I'm late, but I'm here now. Your baby girl is not doing too good. I need you, my right hand." The tears rolled down my face, and my lips trembled as I struggled to get the words out.

I stood there waiting to hear his voice, that thick Jamaican accent to come out and say something. I waited and waited, but nothing happened. That's when it really hit me hard that he wasn't coming back. My baby wasn't coming back to me. My body shivered as I broke down and wept.

"Listen, baby boy, I'm trying to hold on, but it's hard. I should be there wit' you. It's not fair, and I don't want to live without you; I *can't* live without you. Alijah, do you hear me? I can't live without you. I *won't* live without you," I yelled out.

"I love you! I need you, Alijaaah," I screamed as I collapsed on top of the grave.

His cousin Ryan, who was waiting in the car, ran over and picked me up.

"Miss Sierra, is yuh all right, ma'am?"

I could barely respond, so I nodded my head yes. "I just need a few more minutes by myself."

"Yes, ma'am, mi go be right dere waiting."

I know Alijah was dead; at least my mind was telling me that, but my heart wasn't trying to hear that shit. I know he was going to be lonely out here by himself. I didn't want to leave him. I just stood there, shaking uncontrollably.

"Miss Sierra, it's time for us to go, ma'am. My uncle wouldn't want you out here like that, ma'am."

Maybe Ryan was right. What use was it for me to be out here? My Alijah was gone. He helped me back to the car and drove me away. I looked back as the car sped away. I didn't know when I'd be back to see him. I wish he was buried in the States, but I respected the fact that this was his birthplace and his mother wanted him to come home. But was this his home? Alijah's home was with me, in my heart forever.

That night when I got back to the hotel, I went straight to bed. I had a lot on my mind and didn't feel like being bothered. I couldn't stop the tears from flowing, especially when Mama brought me Azir. He looked just like his daddy, and that made it hard for me to cope. I just sat there for hours, looking at my baby. When God made him, he did a complete replica of Alijah's face. Everything about him resembled Alijah. I smiled at him, as I think back on all the good times between his dad and me.

I woke up that morning and decided to let Alijah's mother keep him in Jamaica. Trust me, this wasn't an easy decision for me, but I wasn't in any shape to care for him right now. I need to get my mind right before I can be a good mother to him. I called his grandmother and let her know my decision. She was very pleased and was on her way to get him.

When she got to the hotel, I was sitting there with my baby. I tried to put the best out, but I was dying slowly inside. She decided that she was not going to move back to New York. I think after she lost her son, her love for America was buried along with him.

"Sierra, I really appreciate you doing this. I want you to know I'm going to love and care for your son, my grandson, as if he were mine. You can come visit him anytime you want, and whenever you're ready to get him, I will bring him to you. I know this is the hardest thing you'll ever have to do, and it takes courage. I love you for this and will always be here for you."

She reached over and hugged me. Without any words spoken, we just hugged until Azir realized what was going on and pushed his way in the middle. We both busted out laughing. His little ass was already showing signs of jealousy.

Later that afternoon, Jeanette and I were at Norman Manley International Airport getting ready to board American Airlines back to the United States.

Jeanette kept looking at me crazy. I could tell she wasn't pleased that I was leaving him, but this woman hadn't raised her seed, so her opinion didn't carry much weight with me. I did what was best for my son. I knew he would have the best life with his grandma until I got myself situated; then I'd go back for him. I mean, I wasn't doing this for approval . . . simply for survival.

I held on to Azir as tightly as I could manage. I hugged and kissed him, then handed him to his grandma. The tears rolled down my face, and I didn't want him to see this.

"Say bye-bye to yo' mama."

I couldn't face him, so I didn't turn around and say bye. I didn't want him to see that I was breaking down inside. I pulled my shades out of my purse, put them on, and walked heartbroken to the American Airlines terminal. Once I got on the plane, I put my head in my lap and let it all out. The plane took off, and I was an empty shell sitting down. I was lost and hurt.

"Baby, it's goin' be all right. I don't agree wit' yo' decision, but I respect it. Let's go home." Jeanette rubbed my back and held me the entire flight.

Chapter One

Shayna Jackson

"Fuck you, bitch. You set me up," I spat at the federal bitch. I wasn't in the mood to be cordial to this bitch that thought she was the shit. This bitch was no different than other bitches. I was tired of the feds; they put me in this motherfucking situation, then turned around and fucked me raw!

"Jackson, you better sit your ass down and shut the fuck up. Your ass is in some serious shit. Either you too dumb to understand it, or you just plain stupid."

I had no idea who this lower-class federal bitch was talking to. She must not have seen what happened to the bitch that tried me. I swear these hoes be sleeping on me; they had no idea how deadly I could become.

"Listen, what the fuck am I here for?"

"We're trying to offer you a deal. Your lawyer is on his way up."

"Deal? Bitch, the last time you offered me a deal, I ended up in this hellhole," I yelled.

"I'm not going to be too many more bitches. And, no, honey, you are in here because *you* were too stupid to stay away from the woman your husband was fucking. So, in reality, you're in jail and on your way to prison for life over a dick that you won't ever see again. Now, sit the fuck down before I let them drag yo' ass back to yo' little cell."

I shot that ho a look that could've killed her instantly. This bitch has all the power 'cause she wearing that fucking badge. I know in the real world, this ho wasn't about shit without that damn gun.

"Ha-ha! You think you know me. I never cared about no damn dick, bitch! Matter of fact, I enjoy fucking myself more than any nigga can. No, I'm in here because I require respect at all times and will get it by any means necessary. Bitch, you better watch your back fucking with me." I stared that federal ho down.

"Did you hear that, Counselor? Your client just threatened a federal officer."

"Miss Jackson, please don't say another word. Let me handle this."

"Sure." I smiled at the young, handsome man standing in front of me. I knew it wasn't the right time or place to be thinking about his cock, but I wish I could fuck him. *Oh, well. Soon enough,* I thought.

"Miss Rozzario, what's the purpose of this meeting?"

"The U.S. Attorney's office is offering your client a deal in exchange for her testimony against her husband's codefendants."

"Bitch, fuck you! I will *not* help yo' ass anymore. Don't forget, *I'm* an attorney also. Don't insult my intelligence. Take that deal and shove it up yo' ass. You so big and mighty, take that shit to trial." I got up and looked at her.

"Miss Jackson, sit down! Let's hear them out."

This fool that I was paying had the nerve to fucking yell at me. I looked at him sideways, then back at the federal bitch and the U.S. Attorney. I had a feeling that all these motherfuckers were working against me. I know how the fucking system worked. All these motherfuckers moved around in the same circle. That's why I don't trust them.

I knew that he saw the look on my face that read "Nigga, fuck you." I paid him good money to defend me, not to play pussy and suck up to the fucking enemy. I know I should've defended my damn self.

"So here's what the U.S. Attorney's office is offering. You give us your full cooperation and testify against the two defendants. If, and when, they decide to go to trial, we will recommend thirty years. We'll also let the judge know you cooperated with the court. We will ask for leniency on your part."

"Listen up, Rozzario! I will tell you what you need to know, and I will testify, if needed. But the only way I will do that is if the U.S. Attorney agrees to set me free. If I can't get that, then we have no deal. I'll take my chances with the jurors."

"Counsel, please advise your client her chances of beating the feds are slim to none. We have a 99 percent conviction rate. She better take what we're offering, or her behind will never see these streets again," Rozzario said before she shot me a dirty look with a smile plastered all over her face.

This bitch was really trying me. I wanted to leap across the table and grab that bitch's throat and rip her head off her body. I saw that she was enjoying my misfortune a little bit too much.

"Give us a week to consider your deal. I'm pretty sure she will be more than happy to take you up on your offer," Giovanni smiled.

"Okay, Counselor, don't wait too long. One week, then the deal is off the table."

"Bitch, fuck you! You can shove that shit up yo' ass."

"You will be hearing from us," Giovanni said.

I didn't say another word 'cause this clown was making a fool out of both of us. I stood there with my hands folded. I couldn't wait until I talked to him; I was going to let him know how displeased I was with his incompetent ass. I was ready to go back to the jail, not that I liked it there, but anywhere was better than hearing these idiots discuss my fucking life like I wasn't there.

The guard came and took me back to the holding cell. I welcomed the few minutes of silence. After everything that just went down, I was happy to be alone. I needed to regroup and gather my thoughts. I need to do something fast.

Thirty fucking years. Did I hear this bitch right? I've been in this hellhole for a fucking month, and I was ready to go. I needed to get my damn hair and nails done; I needed to take a few showers. I knew Daddy was turning over in his grave, looking at the treatment his baby girl was getting. The pain of losing him was too much and still hurt everything in me. I really missed him, especially now. Oh, how I wish I could hear his voice telling me it's going to be okay.

"Damn you, Alijah! Why did you have to take my daddy away from me? He's the only man that ever loved me. He loved me through all my flaws," I yelled out.

"Jackson, time to go," the butch-looking bitch yelled and interrupted my thoughts.

Sierra Rogers

By the time, I went through immigration and claimed my bags my phone started to ring. It was my lawyer sounding like he was out of breath.

"Miss Rogers, where are you?"

"I'm just getting back into the country. What's going on?" I stopped and dropped the bags.

"I got a call from a Richmond detective. He wants me to bring you in for questioning."

"Questioning about what?"

"The disappearance of a young lady. I don't have all the details, but I'm on my way there to get more details on what this is all about. I'll call you soon as I get more details."

"A'ight."

I shook my head in disbelief and grabbed the bags. Something is always going on. I'm sick of this fucking shit. I got my mom and me a room and settled in. My mind was all over the place as I nervously waited for the lawyer to call me.

"Sierra, is everything okay? Ever since you got that call at the airport, you seem upset."

"Yes, I'm okay. The police want to question me. Don't ask me about what because I have no idea."

Around 8:00 p.m., my lawyer called. He didn't have anything new. They wanted to talk to me about a friend of mine. After I hung up, I lay under my covers, going over everything in my mind. I know these police were slick, so I needed to make sure my thoughts were well put together. There was no way I was going to let them trip me up into admitting some bullshit.

I was up early. My lawyer told me to meet him at the police station at 11:00 a.m. On my way there, all kinds of thoughts were floating around in my mind. I tried my best to remain calm. I've watched too many crime shows, and I know nervousness is not a good sign. *Breathe, bitch,* I thought as I pulled into the parking lot.

"Hello, my name is Sierra Rogers. My lawyer told me I need to come here for questioning."

Before the woman behind the glass could respond, a dude walked up to me. "Hello, Miss Rogers. I'm Detective Donahue. I believe your lawyer briefed you on why we are meeting here. Please come with me."

I didn't say a damn word. I just looked at him from head to toe. I hated the fucking law, and my hatred for them had gotten even deeper since they killed my man. I knew that I had to watch their slick asses. They're good at switching up people's statements. I also knew that because I was Alijah's woman, they would be trying to tie me up in all his shit. I came prepared for whatever they decided to throw at me.

My lawyer was already seated. Two other pigs were in the room. I took a seat beside my lawyer.

"Miss Rogers, you are one lucky woman. You've survived two attempts on your life," the white pig said.

"I don't think it's luck. I also don't see your concern, because if I'm correct, it was the woman that was working for y'all that tried to kill me while y'all was outside listening," I spat.

"No, ma'am, that's not correct. The feds were the ones that were handling that case, not our office. And to be honest with you, after reading the report, you are not that innocent yourself," he said.

"What the fuck you mean by that?" I looked at him.

"Your dead, drug-dealing boyfriend dragged you into all this chaos. Not us. I'm sure you were well aware of all his illegal activities."

"Listen, Detective whatever the fuck your name is. You know nothing 'bout my man, so watch yo' fucking mouth before you start throwing false accusations out there. Y'all killed him and took him away from his only child. To make matters worse, y'all dragged me in here with some more bullshit. What the fuck y'all really want from me?" At this point, my blood was boiling, and I didn't give a fuck about what might happen.

"Detective, please proceed with this interview. I have other cases to tend to this afternoon, and my client also has things to do."

I love my fucking lawyer. He didn't waste time making small talk.

"Sure. Let's get down to business. Miss Rogers, I'm investigating the disappearance of Neisha Taylor. She's been missing for quite a few months. After doing a thorough investigation, I learned that you two used to be close friends but fell out right before she vanished."

I looked up at this cracker. "So, what are you saying? That's how it is. Sometimes females go through drama, but what does her disappearance have to do with me?"

"It has a lot to do with you. We pulled phone records, and you are one of the last people that she talked to. The victim also told her mother she was meeting up with you."

"I have no idea what you're talking 'bout. So what she called me? We talked for a quick second; then I hung up." I stared him directly in the eyes.

"It doesn't bother you that your friend of over fifteen years just disappeared into thin air?"

"Since you did yo' homework, Detective, you already know that Neisha and I were no longer friends. Before that phone call, I hadn't seen her in months." I didn't flinch one bit.

"Miss Rogers, we are fresh into the investigation, and I owe an explanation to her poor mother, who just wants to know what happened to her daughter. May I ask, what was it you and she discussed in that brief phone conversation?"

"I can't recall. But it wasn't nothing important. I was busy, so I hung up."

"If I'm correct, y'all are childhood friends, right?" he looked at me.

"We used to be friends, Detective, and as I said, we were no longer friends. Well, I hope you find your answer, but as you can see, you're barking up the wrong tree. I have nothing to do with Neisha or her disappearance. So it seems like you should be out there searching for her."

"Maybe, but I have a good feeling about this. Your boyfriend is dead, but you're still here, and trust me, soon as I gather more information and evidence, I *will* be coming for you," he said and winked at me.

"Unless you're charging my client with something, we are leaving. Detective, you have my number; please don't hesitate to call. I advise you and your department to stay away from my client. If y'all keep it up, I will slap Richmond PD with a harassment lawsuit."

"Ha-ha. I hear you, Counselor. Make sure you stay on that payroll, 'cause I'm coming. Have a good day, folks."

"Let's go, Miss Rogers. We're finished here."

I walked out the door with my attorney following close by.

"They have nothing on you. He's just trying to rattle you a bit. Basically, he's trying to dig."

"Dig for what? I don't know shit 'bout that woman's disappearance."

"Trust me, if they had any evidence, they would've charged you. All they have is the phone record showing the woman contacted you on the same day she disappeared. I think you should go on 'bout your business and not worry 'bout a thing."

"Yeah, but I'm mad as hell. This fucking police department is trying to get me caught up in some bullshit. Call me if you hear anything else."

"Okay, Miss Rogers. You look like hell. Get some rest and don't worry yourself."

I walked off toward the parking garage. I put on a good show in front of them, but deep down, I was shivering. Only three of us knew what went down. Two were dead, and I wasn't talking. I ain't got shit to say. I knew Alijah's boys helped him to clean up the mess, but I wasn't worried about them talking either. I quickly walked to my car. My head was pounding. I just needed to lie down. I had so many things to take care of, but lately, I couldn't seem to focus. During the daytime I was fine, but at night, I can't sleep. I've been popping Percocet and Xanax to help me through the rough times.

"Why did you leave me, Alijah? I need you more than ever," I said as I drove down Broad Street.

I stopped by the salon to see Mo' and to let her know that I was leaving. I made up my mind the previous night to get out of Virginia. I used to have mad love for Richmond, but after all that went down, I could no longer live here; too many memories of Alijah. Besides, since he died, Jeanette and I have been living in the hotel because the feds took the house.

I wasn't tripping; I had no intention to live in that house anymore. Everything inside reminded me of him.

I smiled as I recalled the day when Alijah first brought me around there. The feeling of happiness that I felt. I thought we would have some good memories, but instead, he was gone, and all I was left with was pain and anger.

"Hey, boo," I greeted Mo'.

"Hey, love. I tried to call you earlier."

"Girl, my phone was turned off. Then as soon as we landed, my lawyer told me that the fucking detectives wanted me fo' questioning."

"What! For what? Bitch, don't tell me them motherfuckers fucking with you 'cause of Alijah shit."

"For Neisha. These motherfuckers think I got something to do with her disappearing."

"Bitch, nah. What in the world would make them think that? You been through enough as it is. You don't need to be dragged into no damn investigation. They need to be looking at the fucking dope boys. That bitch might owe them money. I mean, I feel bad and all 'cause we grew up wit' the bitch, but fuck her; she's a snake."

"Girl, I don't know what happened to the bitch, and I couldn't care less if she's dead or not. That bitch betrayed me by givin' an outside bitch info on me. She lucky I didn't kill her when I had the chance."

"They tryin'a fuck with you 'cause of Alijah's situation. They embarrassed that an outside nigga made a fool out of their city and made a fool out of them."

"When does this shit end? I'm tired, for real. Sometimes, I just want to crawl into a hole and stay there. Mo', I'm tired for real."

"Listen, bitch, I can't say I understand, 'cause I've never been in your situation. I do know you're one strong bitch, and the Sierra I know would not talk like this. You'll be a'ight soon; give it time, boo."

"I hear you, Mo'; I'm trying. Some days are better than others. I miss my man terribly; sometimes at night, I lie down, and as soon as I close my eyes, I see him. I want to touch him. I want to tell him I love him one last time, but I can't, 'cause he's not really there. It's my fucking mind playing tricks on me."

"Yeah, boo, it's your mind fucking with you 'cause you and him have a connection. You was his ride or die, and I wouldn't be surprised if his spirit followed yo' ass back from Jamaica." She busted out laughing.

I sat there in silence. I knew no one would understand the pain I was in, not because they were not trying, but simply because unless it had happened to them, they couldn't tell how much it hurt. I felt so lost without my soul mate.

"So, I got something to tell you."

"What, bitch? This sound serious." She shot me a strange look.

"I'm moving. I'm leaving Virginia."

"You're leaving? Bitch, stop playing."

"I'm dead-ass serious. I'm thinking about moving down South; maybe Atlanta. I heard houses out there are cheaper. Plus, I plan on opening another shop eventually."

"When did you come up with this idea?" she asked as she side-eyed me.

"I've been thinking about it ever since I got out of the hospital in Jamaica. Mo', there's nothing in Richmond for me anymore. Azir is going to live with me soon, and I can't raise him up here. The streets don't love them young boys, and I already lost his father. I can't risk losing my son also."

"Damn, bitch, you act like I'm not here. I mean, we're not blood, but I thought we shared something special."

"Damn, Mo', this ain't about you. I need to do this for me. You'll always be my partner, and we can visit each other. You acting like I'm moving to another continent or some shit like that."

"Yeah . . . You know what, Sierra? I've been patiently waiting for over a year. I stuck by yo' side through everything. Good or bad, right or wrong. You call, I'm there. Now, you pop up in here, telling me you leaving. Something ain't right about this shit."

"And I thought that's what friends are for, right?" I looked at her for reassurance.

"Sierra, cut the bullshit out. I'm not talking about no friendship."

"I'm lost. What the hell *are* you talking about, Mo'?"

"I mean, Sierra, you know I like you more than just your best friend. I want us to be together. I want to be your bitch, and you my bitch. I want a relationship."

"Bitch, you trippin'. You know I'm not gay, and what you mean you want us to be together?"

"So, I'm good enough to suck on your pussy, but I'm not good enough to be with?"

"Mo', come on, girl, you trippin'. We did what we did, but I've kept it real with you from day one. I could never be with a woman. I love dick too damn much. After I get my pussy ate, I be wanting to be fucked by a man. I don't know 'bout anybody and how they live their life, but it's just not for me; not every day anyway. I just can't do it. Plus, you my best friend."

"You keep wasting your time on these no-good-ass niggas when I'm right here. I love you, Sierra, and can make you happy. I watched how that nigga dogged you out, and I was there when you was hurting. C'mon, ma."

"Mo', I came to you because you my bitch. I never knew you was on some personal shit. Yes, we fucked around, but that's all it was. I love you as my right-hand bitch, but I'm not *in* love with you."

"I feel you. I'm not trippin'. You still my ace, no matter what."

I saw the look of disappointment plastered across her face. I didn't mean to say it to hurt her, but I had to keep it one hundred with her. There was no hope of us being together, only because it wasn't my thing. That would be too much pussy rubbing going on, without any kind of dick in the middle. I'm not a ho, but I love getting fucked by a man.

"Am I? 'Cause you just went off the deep end on me just now. When did you get so strung out on pussy? I know you was bi, but you giving up dick is crazy."

"Who said I was giving up dick? I just thought since we did everything together, we might as well *be* together. Like I said, no sweat; you my bitch, and that ain't gonna change."

"It better not. I appreciate you being in my life. I don't know what I would do without you. Me moving to another state doesn't mean shit. You might even decide to come on down there."

"Nah, boo, I'm good. I live and breathe Richmond, baby, and I ain't going nowhere."

"I hear you, but on some real shit, please be careful out here. Don't trust these bitches or these niggas."

"Sierra, these niggas know better. They know who my brothers are. Anything happens to me, trust me, it's going to be bloodshed all over the city."

"I'm good; just take care of yourself and know I'm only a phone call away," I said.

"Bitch, I'm going to miss your crazy ass. Come here let me show you how much."

Mo' inched closer to me and started to massage my shoulders. She knew damn well that was my weakness. Before I knew it, our lips were locked together. We kissed passionately for a few minutes. Mo's hand made its way up under my dress, and she pulled my drawers down. She stuck her finger inside my already-moist pussy. The feeling of her soft hand on my clit sent me into a sexual frenzy.

"No, wait; you forgot you're at work," I mumbled.

Mo' stepped away, closed the blinds, then locked the door. She grabbed my hand and led me into the back office.

"The door is locked, and no one is coming 'til later. Relax and let me please you."

She pushed me onto the sofa, spread my legs apart, and placed them on her shoulders. That's when her tongue made contact with my clit. Mo' had a way of gently licking my clit that drove me insane.

"Oh . . . ooh," I groaned and moaned.

I used my hand to give her head an extra push into my sweet pussyhole. I tried to rub on her breasts, but I couldn't focus. She ate my pussy so damn good, I had multiple orgasms; I came all over her face. Until then, I had not realized how backed up I was. I was going through so much that sex was the last thing on my mind, I guess. To clean my pussy juice off her face, I grabbed some paper towels that were nearby and wet them. I wiped myself off, then grabbed my boy shorts.

"Damn, boo, that ass gettin' fatter." She slapped me on the butt.

"I don't know how. I lost a shitload of weight. Most of my clothes falling off me. I need a new wardrobe."

"Yeah, you might've lost weight, but that pussy still fat and juicy."

"Girl, shut up! You're too damn wide open. OMG."

"Sierra, you are an undercover freak, and you are in denial that you love pussy. Not me, I love pussy and dick. Best of both worlds."

"I'm not undercover anything. You turned me out. I guess you tryin'a have me gone off the head, but no, boo-boo. I love dick. Big, black, thick, juicy dick all up in my pussy," I teased.

"I got a big black dildo for that ass."

"Fuck you, bitch! I don't want no plastic. If I ever want to get fucked, it would be with a real dick with veins."

"Yeah, yeah, whatever. I'm not listening to none of that shit you talking 'bout. You are still a newbie. In a few years, you'll be telling me how much you love pussy."

"Bitch, bye. I got to go. I need to let Jeanette know my plans."

"So, you taking Jeanette with you?"

"I mean, I'm about to let her know my plans. If she wants to go, then she can go. It's cool by me if she don't want to go."

"You really think Jeanette going to leave Richmond?"

"I don't see why not. She ain't got nobody but me. Like I said, she's grown."

"You right, boo."

"Aye, Mo', so I want you to run this shop. I mean, we can split the profit. I will still pay to keep it running, but you will be here."

"Well, you know, I'm fine with that. Most of the customers already think we're partners anyway."

I stayed a little while longer so we could discuss business. I was taking most of the money that was in the business account. I knew it was hard starting over, but I was ready to start over fresh and get away from all the bad memories this city had brought to my family and me.

Chapter Two

Shayna Jackson

"Jackson, get up! You have an attorney's visit," the big black CO bitch yelled into my cell.

I jumped up off my bunk, slipped on my shower shoes, and walked out of my cell. I glanced up at the clock and noticed it was a little past 9:00 a.m. It was a little early for an attorney's visit, but I was eager to see this fool after the way he clowned the other day in front of the feds.

"Good morning, Miss Jackson."

I rolled my eyes and sat in the chair across from him at the table in the lawyer-client visitation room.

"It's early for a visit. You must have some good news for me."

"Today is the deadline that the feds gave us. The plea will be off the table by 5:00 p.m. today."

"I told yo' ass and them that I wasn't interested in no goddamn deal unless it was me walking out of these fucking doors."

"Miss Jackson, you're playing a dangerous game. I'm one of the best at what I do, but you already know that. With that said, I'm letting you know if we don't accept this plea deal and we go to trial, you're looking at life imprisonment. You're charged with some serious crimes, and the feds are very upset that you committed these crimes on their watch."

"I hired you to defend me, so I don't give a fuck about the feds' feelings. They fucking used me and left me for dead. Do your fucking job and get me out of here."

"As an attorney yourself, you should know it's not that easy to beat a federal case. I filed some motions on your behalf, so I'm waiting to hear back from them. As your attorney, I suggest that we take the plea deal and ask for leniency. You have a better chance of getting out in little to no time. Your criminal history level is zero, so that plays into how much time you'll get."

"Listen to you. This entire conversation is based on *me* doing time. Not one time did I hear you say when *I get off*. You have no confidence in this case."

"Miss Jackson, I'm in this with you 100 percent, but as your attorney, I have to advise you of the worst possible scenario. You're the boss, so if you want to go to trial, then that's what we will do."

I sat quietly for a few minutes. I was playing out in my head all the different ways this case could go. My head was telling me to tell the feds to fuck off, but my heart was telling me to think like an attorney. I knew all too well about plea deals. That was how I got most of my clients off. I knew the feds were trying to make an example out of me, and I wasn't going to play into that trap.

"Take the deal."

"What the hell just happened? First, you're against it; then, out of the blue, you're telling me to take the deal?"

"Make no misunderstanding. I'm mad as fuck, but I can't risk going to prison for the rest of my life. They think they have the last laugh, but trust me when I tell you, Shayna Jackson *always* gets what she wants."

"Okay . . . I'm going to head on over to the U.S. Attorney's office. Give me a call this evening, and I'll let you know where we stand."

I noticed while we were talking, his eyes kept shifting to my breasts. That thought alone made my pussy jump. It's been awhile since I had some dick, and I would love to ride him, right here in the office.

"Gotcha. Let me ask you a quick question. Do you ever get hard when you stare at my breasts?"

"Excuse me?"

"You heard me. I see the way you stare at my chest and how you look at me with lust in your eyes. C'mon, tell me, does your cock gets hard for me?"

"Miss Jackson, you're undoubtedly a gorgeous woman, but it's strictly professional between us."

"Sure. I'll be home soon. I would love to see how that cock feels up inside me," I said while I rubbed his hand and winked at him.

"Have a good day, Mrs. Jackson."

I smiled at him and watched as he grabbed his briefcase and walked out the door. I know that nigga's dick was hard, and he had to hurry up out of here.

I walked past the boys' pod, and those thirsty motherfuckers started hollering and whistling. Boy, I tell you, they're behaving as if they were not used to a bad bitch. The thirst was real, but they were hollering at the wrong bitch. These bums didn't have enough money to afford me even on my worst day.

By the time I got back to the cell, all the loud-ass bitches were up. God knew that it killed me every day to be around these low-level bitches. I was especially sick of my bunkie; that ho farted and snored like a fucking man. I never imagined that a woman could be that fucking disgusting.

There were nights when I thought of strangling that ho, but I tried hard not to snap 'cause I was trying to go home.

Then there were the bitches that sucked on each other every day. A few days ago, one had the nerve to call herself trying to get with me. It was one of those big, burly, black bitches. I had to shut that ho down fast. Another bitch's pussy didn't interest me. Shit, what kind of pleasure would I have gotten out of rubbing pussy with another bitch? Then that bitch had the nerve to catch an attitude; she walked off mumbling something under her breath.

It was a circus in the jail. If you sat around long enough, you'd hear these low-level bitches claim to be bad bitches, drug dealers, and rich bitches. I sat back and smiled; these hoes were fronting, trying to be important. Bullshit—most of these hoes used to cook crack for the dope boys, while others were human mules, transporting drugs from state to state. It was sad because now that their asses were locked up, they couldn't even afford a lawyer or get a dollar on their books. Bad bitches! More like poor bitches. I need to teach these bitches some game, I thought.

I lay in my cell thinking about my next move . . . Whatever it was, it had to be my best move!

***

Six weeks later after pleading guilty, I was standing in front of a cracker judge for sentencing. My guideline was 360–480 months. I whispered a prayer to Daddy, asking him to watch over his baby girl. I needed him more than ever. I know I ain't did a lot of good in my lifetime, but my daddy did.

The U.S. Attorney stood up and addressed the court. Nothing he said surprised me one bit; however, he did ask for the lower end of my sentencing guideline.

"Mrs. Jackson, do you want to address this court before we move on?"

"No, Your Honor. I ain't got nothing to say."

I wasn't in the mood to kiss their asses. After how the feds used me, then threw me under the bus by locking my ass up, I had little hope in the judicial system, and I didn't think by me saying a few words, my fate was going to be changed. That cracker already had his mind made up.

"Well, Miss Jackson, I've read your case, and I also had a chance to talk to the pretrial officer. The crime of attempted murder that you committed against this young lady was very heinous. You must pay for your actions. I now sentence you to 360 months in a federal facility and five years' supervised release upon completion of your prison sentence. I order you to undergo mental health counseling while incarcerated," the old fuck that could barely speak above a whisper said.

Sierra Rogers

This was one of the best days I'd had since all hell broke loose—the sentencing of that wicked bitch that ruined my life. I was mad as hell when I heard they offered her a plea deal. I had no understanding of how this bitch tried to kill me twice and *still* managed to get a fucking deal.

I lost confidence in the justice system. They took my man away, and now they're giving this rat-ass bitch a fucking deal so she can come out and become an earth disturber again. I'm not even going to say what I was going to do if our paths ever crossed again; it's not going to be anything good. That bitch deserves to rot in prison and never walk these streets again.

I walked into the courtroom just in time to hear the U.S. Attorney's statement. I couldn't believe that I was sitting in the same room with this evil bitch. Our eyes locked, and she smiled at me. I wish I could've gotten to her because they would've been picking her face up off the floor.

The judge then called me up to say something before he sentenced her. My heart was racing. My hands were sweaty. I got up and walked to the front. As I walked past Shayna's bitch ass, I stared her down with a long, cold stare. I was trying to let this bitch know. She got lucky once again.

I made sure I looked directly at the judge while I spoke. "Your Honor, all I have to say is, Miss Jackson is an evil woman that has a personal vendetta against me. She tried to kill me, not once, but twice, over a man. I've never provoked or done anything to harm this woman, but her only intention was to kill me. Your Honor, my life will never be the same; I've endured mental and physical pain all because of this woman." I paused, wiped my tears, then continued.

"I beg the courts, Your Honor, to impose the stiffest sentence on her."

I felt relieved after I got that out of my system. This was one time I hope the judge will do the right thing.

"Thank you, Miss Rogers. This court will take into consideration all that you've been through. You may step down."

I walked off the stand and looked at that ho. Only this time, her stupid ass wasn't laughing anymore. She sat there looking like a lost puppy.

"Ms. Jeanette Rogers, you also want to address the court. Please step up."

"Good morning, Judge, Your Honor. As a mother, I can't explain the feeling that I felt when Sierra got shot. All I can remember, I knelt down on the ground holding my only child. I remember begging God not to take her away from me. My chest started tightening up on me. I couldn't breathe. Your Honor, I warned my daughter that something wasn't right about that woman, but she didn't listen. What made it even worse, after she shot my child, she laughed; she was *happy* that she was dying. I beg you, Your Honor, please give her the maximum sentence because she needs to learn a lesson. She needs to not ever walk these streets again. Not ever," Jeanette pleaded to the judge with tears rolling down her face.

The judge gave that bitch thirty years in prison. I was outraged. They should have given her life, but she was given that time because of the plea that they offered her in exchange for testifying against Alijah's boys. I felt so bad for them. Because of their loyalty to Alijah, they also got caught up in this bitch's web of deceit. Now with this bitch getting ready to testify against them, they had no chance of seeing the streets again. So many lives lost because of this wicked bitch!

Everything happened so fast! The judge sentenced her ass; I looked up, and this ho done fainted. I was hoping she was dead, but I heard someone holler, "They got a pulse." I guess her ass wasn't so tough after all. I didn't stick around to see what happened to her. Jeanette and I made our exit as the EMTs entered the courtroom. I had better things to do than sit around and watch this foolery!

Exactly two weeks later, I was packed and was on the road to Atlanta, Georgia. I had contacted a real estate agent out there and learned that the houses were pretty cheap. I had a list of them to look at when I got there. I didn't want anything huge; a three-bedroom was fine; one bedroom for me, one for Jeanette, and one for Azir. I was happy that I had money stashed away because after losing everything, I don't know what I would have done. *I can't imagine living forever without you, Alijah. You spoiled me and gave me the finest of everything and your love.* It kind of hurts thinking about it, because I would trade anything in this world to have him back.

"You all right, baby girl?" Jeanette interrupted my thoughts.

"Yeah. Just hard leaving the one place I know, but I'm good."

"Well, look at it like this. Your memories will always be with you. It's not easy, but you are doing what's best for you."

"I guess so," I said.

Yes, it's true that I wanted to leave Richmond because of everything that went down, but the main cause was a detective's investigation. I've been praying every day that God would let it all go away. I can't picture me doing time in prison behind that bitch. Alijah assured me that they would never find the body because it was gone. I knew he was on top of his shit, so I can only hope that the police were just fishing.

Jeanette and I didn't talk much on the ride. We were both lost in our thoughts. I tried not to put a lot of stress on her, because I knew she was an addict and stress could trigger a relapse. I knew I wouldn't know how to deal with her if she was on crack again. My life was already fucked up; I couldn't take anymore.

After making a stop in Charlotte, North Carolina, and again in Greenville, South Carolina, I saw a sign that read: WELCOME TO GEORGIA. I knew we were almost there, and I let out a long breath as I drove into my future.

We stayed in a hotel for 'bout a month. Every day we were out house hunting. I swear my ass looked at over twenty houses. This was harder than I thought it would be. I finally found a house that grabbed my attention. It wasn't as big as my previous house, but it was nice. I told the realtor that I wanted it, and he handled everything else. The process was very easy 'cause I paid cash. Jeanette and I were both happy because we're tired of living in the hotel.

It took us a few weeks for everything to get finalized; then we were able to move into the house. It took us no time to get the things out of storage and get ourselves settled. It felt like home again after we decorated it the way we wanted it. I thought I could finally get some sleep at night. Ever since I'd been shot, sleep became my worst enemy. The pain in my head was unbearable and seeing Alijah's cold, stiff body in the coffin made my pain worse. At first, I was taking the prescribed dosage of Percocet, but the pain became more intense; it was to the point where I used to lie in my bed crying. I started popping pills like I used to do the first time I got shot. My doctor noticed that I was coming to him too early for refills. He advised me that I should slow down and seek some help. I didn't think I had a problem, so I told him okay, grabbed my prescription from him, and walked out of the office.

That didn't stop anything; I found two other doctors that I started to visit. After explaining to them how much pain I was in, it took them no time to write me a prescription for the same ailments. The extra pills from those doctors helped the physical part of the pain. I was constantly high every day, all day. I ain't going to lie; not only was it helping my physical pain, but it was also helping my mental pain. I didn't cry as much as I used to when I was back in Richmond, but I also realized the more I popped the pills, the more dependent I was becoming.

After a month of doing nothing but eating and hanging around the house, I decided it was time for me to get shit in order. I got up extra early this morning because I had an appointment with my real estate dude. I was looking to buy a salon. After not being able to work for a while, I felt like it was time to step back into reality. I've been living off my savings, and I knew if I didn't have any income coming in, it would only be a matter of time before my money would start getting low. Alijah had money stashed away for Azir, but I didn't want to touch it. Not now, anyway, until I was sure the feds didn't know anything about it. I knew this wasn't how Alijah intended for it to

be. If he were here, he'd make sure that I didn't
want for anything, but the cold, harsh reality
was that he was gone, and I was still here.

I wasn't trippin' because I was a go-getter,
and I was going to get mines by any means
necessary. I took a shower and was about to get
dressed when I rushed back to the bathroom. I
kept trying to vomit, even though my stomach
was empty. I couldn't stop the dry heaving. I
hated it when this would happen because all
that came up was some green, nasty liquid. My
chest started to hurt every time I tried to throw
up, and my eyes filled with tears as I knelt down
beside the toilet. I knew what I needed: my pills,
which were downstairs in my pocketbook. I
managed to wash out my mouth, then opened
the bathroom door.

"Sierra, we need to talk."

"Talk 'bout what? Something wrong?"

"Yes, something is terribly wrong."

"And what's that?" I pushed past her.

I had a feeling where this conversation was
heading, and God knows I wasn't in the fucking
mood.

"Sierra, fo' months, I've watched you, and I see
some of the same signs that I had when I was
doing drugs."

"You're accusing me of being a crackhead?" I
stopped dead in my tracks.

"No, not crack. Hell, I'm not sure what it is, but my guess is it's those painkillers that you've been taking."

"The doctor prescribed those."

"They might've, but you are becoming too dependent on them. I listen to how angry you get when you don't take them; then right after you take them, your mood changes to happy and playful. I know those signs, Sierra."

"Oh, that's right. I forgot I was talkin' to a junkie, but just because you're one, that doesn't make me one, Mother," I said sarcastically.

"Sierra, you see how you behaving right now? It just confirmed that I'm right."

"Listen, lady! I don't want to disrespect you, so please worry 'bout yo' fuckin' self. Last time I checked, I was grown and don't need to explain myself to no fucking body," I said as I stormed downstairs.

I thought this lady would have gotten the picture and left me the fuck alone, but no, this crackhead, dopefiend, selling-pussy-ass bitch followed me downstairs.

"Sierra, listen to me. You need to seek help before it's too late. What's going to happen when these pills can't stop the pain anymore? I know the next step up is heroin, and, baby girl, that ain't nothing nice to play with."

"Listen, bitch, please leave me the fuck alone before I put you out of my shit. Yo' ass should be somewhere up in somebody's NA meeting. Remember, *you* are a crackhead. *You* need the fucking help; if not, you're going to be around here with a glass dick in yo' mouth, fuckin' and suckin' every nasty-ass dick that comes your way."

"I'm not even going to respond to you. Trust me, I accept that I was a piece of shit of a mother, and I accept everything that you dish out to me. As much as I hate the things that you say to me, I know it's the truth, so I don't say too much. But before you go pointing fingers at me, go look in the fucking mirror and see how different you are. You may not be a crackhead, but you sure are on your way to something stronger than pills. Yes, I left you when I felt like I couldn't take care of you, but how are you so different? It's been months since you took Azir down to the islands, and he *still* there. I beg you every day to get your baby, so you won't walk the same path I went down. Look at me; I'm damn near fifty with nothing. No education and no car. Nothing."

I took a step closer to her face . . . Then I spoke.

"I'll *never* be you. I didn't just up and leave my baby. He's with his grandma, and I've been through a fuckin' lot. *That's* why I haven't gone to get him as yet. Bitch, don't you ever accuse me of not being there for mine. I will *never* be you. I call my child every damn day. I send him money every damn week. When you left me, did you do any of that? Hell nah. Bitch, you left me for dead," I said and stormed off to get my pocketbook.

That bitch just ripped my heart into tiny pieces, but I wouldn't dare show any emotion in front of her. I grabbed my Michael Kors purse and pranced upstairs, went into my room, and slammed the door behind me. I snatched up the bottle of Percocet, went to the bathroom, and washed them down with the sink water. I sat on my bed with tears rolling down my cheeks, feeling like I wanted to crawl into a hole instead of being there. I was mad at her for pointing out my flaws, but who was she to judge me? Only God knows the mental and physical pain I was experiencing. I started to bawl uncontrollably; I didn't want to go on anymore. I grabbed the pill bottle again, went into the bathroom, and swallowed all of them. I wasn't sure how many I swallowed, but in a quick second, I regretted my stupid decision. I walked into my room and crawled back into my bed, totally forgetting the reason I was up so early in the first place. Instead, I pulled the cover over me as my thoughts became distant, and I started to drift off to sleep.

"Sierra, open the door," I heard someone yelling from what appeared to be far away.

I tried to mumble something to let the person know I wasn't feeling well, but the sound diminished and my voice trailed off . . .

"Sierra, please hang on, baby. The ambulance is on the way. Please, baby, I didn't mean to upset you." Jeanette's voice sounded like it was far away. I tried keeping my eyes open, but I was sleepy. *I just need to sleep,* I thought.

I ended up in the hospital again. This time, I was forced to drink charcoal. The taste was horrible, but I quickly downed the bottle. The doctor informed me that the shrink was coming to interview me. This shit was getting out of hand, and I had no idea how to stop it.

Jeanette sat in the chair across from my bed. She wore a disgusted look on her face. I don't know why, because she didn't have to be here. I was grown, and I could handle whatever was thrown at me.

I was still feeling weak and disoriented. I wanted to cry, but I used all my might to keep it all in.

"You don't have to be here. You can go home."

"Sierra, you need to calm yo' damn nerves. I'm here because I chose to be."

Before I could respond, a tall, white woman walked in. "Hello, Miss Rogers. I'm Doctor Blackwell."

"Hi."

"Can you please excuse us? I would like to talk to the patient in private."

"Sure," Jeanette said before she walked out.

"So tell me what's going on with you. You came to us via ambulance because you overdosed on prescription pills."

"I don't know what happened. I was upset and felt like I wanted to die, so I took the pills."

I could've lied, but honestly, I was tired and had hit rock bottom. I was sick and tired of being sick and tired. My life had spiraled downhill over the past year, from me getting shot twice to Alijah going to jail, to him getting killed. This was too fucking much for one person.

"Did you want to harm yourself or others?"

"I don't know what I was thinking. I just wanted to die," I busted out bawling.

"Here's some tissue. I'll give you a few seconds to get yourself together." She handed me a box of Kleenex.

After I got the crying under control, I gave her the rundown of what was going on with me. It wasn't easy letting a total stranger in my business, but I'm glad I did.

"Listen, lady, I got shot twice within a year by a bitch that was crazy, and that wasn't the worst. You know what the worst is? My man and the love of my life getting killed by the fucking police. They didn't have to kill him. He was a good man," I cried.

"I'm sorry about all that you had to go through, but how did that make you feel?"

"Make me feel?"

"Yes, are you angry at the police? Do you want to hurt them?"

This ho was trying to set me up. I might be at my lowest, but I wasn't totally gone.

"No, I'm just fucking angry. I just want him back. I want to tell him one last thing."

The more I let it out, the better I was starting to feel. I didn't give a fuck if that cracker bitch sat on her mighty throne judging me. Shit, if she ever experienced half the shit that I've been through, she would have downed more than just pills.

"Okay, Miss Rogers. After listening to you, it's my professional expertise that you are experiencing a mental breakdown. It's not rare for a person that's experienced the kind of trauma that you described. I also believe you have an addiction to pain medication. I want to admit you to our in-patient psychiatric department. That way, you can get the help that you need."

"What the fuck you mean? I ain't fucking crazy."

"You are correct. You're not crazy, but you are going through a difficult time, and you need professional help. I'll ask your mother to sign your admission papers so we can get you the help you need."

She didn't wait for a response; instead, she walked out of the room. Seconds later, she returned with Jeanette.

"Miss Rogers, I was telling your daughter that I would ask your permission to have her admitted to the psychiatric unit."

I shot Jeanette a look. *This bitch done lost her mind if she agreed to some bullshit like this,* I thought.

"Well, baby, you need the help, and the only way you gonna get it is if you stay in here."

"What? Who the fuck died and made you the fucking chief of my motherfucking life?"

"Calm down, Miss Rogers. Your mother is only trying to do what's best for you. No need to get upset; it's only temporary."

"Really? You're going to let a crackhead bitch decide if I should be admitted? I'm grown as fuck, and I'm getting up outta here." I sat up on the bed.

"I'm afraid you can't do that! The way you're behaving, you're not only a danger to yourself, but also to others."

I watched as she radioed for help. This white bitch was really performing. That's what my ass got for running my mouth, telling this bitch my business. I saw what was happening; this bitch didn't come here to help me. She knew all along what she was going to do.

I looked at Jeanette and shook my head. This bitch had no idea what she had done, but she'd find out soon as I got up out of there. Before I knew it, my ass was hauled off to the psych unit. It was cold as an icebox. I shivered as I sat there in one of those straitjackets. I was stripped of my clothing, which made it one of the most humiliating times of my life. So I lost my rights and my dignity all in one day, I thought. If they thought I wanted to kill myself earlier, this only made it worse.

I tried to doze off, but the coldness prevented me from doing so. I sat up and wrapped my hands around my knees.

"Chile," I heard a warm, soft voice say.

I jumped up, only to see the all-too-familiar face smiling down at me.

"Nana, you startled me. What you're doing here? I thought I would never see you again."

"You should know by now that wherever you go, I'm always a few steps behind." She gave me a slight smile. "Chile, you listen to me. I need you to dig yo'self out of this pit that you're in."

"I 'ont know how. I'm feeling too weak," I cried.

She took a few steps closer and sat beside me. "You have to. You the only one that can do it. Reach down in your soul and dig for your inner strength."

I didn't respond; instead, I sat there crying.

"Dry them damn tears! Take this time you're in here and get your strength back. This is for your own good. God didn't bring you this far to leave you."

"It's easy for you to say. I just wanna die."

"Foolishness! Chile, you're not a quitter. Get your shit in order and fight for you and that baby."

"I—" before I could finish my sentence, I looked beside me, and she was gone.

Great! She's also upset with me too, I thought.

I sat there crying and pondering what she said to me. This was my second time seeing my nana. It was always times when I felt like I wanted to give up. That lady never left me, not spiritually.

***

I realized fighting these people was not going to get me released any faster. So I was obliged to everything they wanted me to do. I had to do group counseling twice a week and individual counseling every day. The doctor decided he didn't want to put me on any other medication just yet because I was addicted to painkillers. I had to admit that after about two weeks of no painkillers, I *was* feeling better. My emotions were not all over the place like they used to be, and I was coping better with the loss of Alijah. Talking with the counselors also helped me to come to terms with why I harbor so much anger toward Jeanette. This was my first time letting anyone dig deep into my thoughts. It hurt at first to talk about everything I went through. But the more I did it, the easier it became.

Six weeks later, I was walking out of the psych unit. As I exited the floor and entered the lobby, I noticed Jeanette sitting down. Going in, I was mad at her, but I was happy to see her face now. She ran over to me and hugged me. I hugged her back.

"How you feeling, baby girl? You look good."

"Better," I smiled.

"You look better. You even gained a few pounds. Your face looks refreshed. Skin looks clear. Come on; I drove your car. It's parked across the street. Parking up here is crazy."

I was going to ask why she was driving my shit, but I decided not to. I was still a little bit salty at her for signing those fucking papers. I got into the passenger side and rolled my window down. I welcomed the fresh air because I was used to the smell of Pine-Sol that they used daily to mop the floors.

"You hungry?"

"I'm starved. I need some real food. Stop by that Jamaican restaurant; I believe the name is Travellers, by Glenwood. I'm feigning for some curry chicken, peas, and rice."

"Sounds good, 'cause I'm too damn tired to cook."

After getting my food, I pushed back my seat and disappeared into my thoughts. I was trying to figure out where I was heading from this point on. The pain was buried deep down, but after weeks of getting counseled, I think I had it figured out, and I'd learned how to deal with my emotional pain a little better. As for my physical pain, the doctor took me off the Percocet and prescribed Ibuprofen 800 mg instead. It didn't work as well as the Percocet, but I took it anyway.

"We're home," Jeanette said, interrupting my thoughts.

I was happy to be home finally. I got out of the car and tried to haul ass upstairs, but Jeanette grabbed my arm.

"Sierra, I know you might still be upset with me because I signed those papers. Please understand that it was out of love. I've been there, and I didn't want to see you head down the same path. Addiction is a sickness that is not easy. Look at me. I struggle e'eryday just to stay clean."

"I'm tired. I need to shower and crawl into my bed," I said and walked off.

The first thing I did was jump into the shower. I stood still and allowed the water to pound my body. I then used my Olay Body Wash to erase weeks of grime off my body. In the midst of bathing, I busted out crying. I let it all out in the shower. The water and my tears ran down into the drain alongside the soap suds.

I got out and dried myself off, lotioned my skin, and put on my favorite pajamas. They were my favorites because Alijah bought them for me. Every time I used to put them on, he would say, "Damn, ma, yo' ass phat as fuck!" I would smile back at him and say, "Boy, quit playing! My ass phat all the time." I cracked a smile as I remembered the good times we had. There were also bad times, but deep down, he was a good man who got caught up in the streets. I recalled times when I would beg him to leave the streets alone, but who was I kidding? Alijah lived and breathed the same streets that got him killed. And because of that, I'd lost my lover and my best friend.

I wish I could change the hands of time, but I knew it wasn't possible. I planned to get my son back and make sure he didn't end up like his father. God knows I couldn't bear the pain . . .

I was ready to get things rolling again, and this time, I was feeling better mentally and physically. I think getting out of the house and working will keep my mind occupied. I hit up the realtor again, apologized for my missed appointment, and set up a new appointment. I let him know what I was looking for, and I needed something as soon as possible.

Within two months, I officially opened a new salon on South Hairston Road. This shop was a full-scale salon; I had a section for hair, nails, and I hired a certified massage therapist. It was a one-stop shop. Starting over wasn't easy, but I gave out flyers at the grocery stores, Walmart parking lots, and wherever else I went. The day of the grand opening, I was very nervous. This was a new environment for me, and the area was already swamped with beauty salons. I was confident in my skills, so I knew it was only a matter of getting the word around town.

I've always wanted to do it big! The people of Stone Mountain came out and showed out. I offered a discount, and the other stylist and I worked our asses off that day. It was well past midnight when the last client walked out. By the time I got to the house, my feet were swollen, and my body felt like I'd taken a serious ass whooping.

Jeanette was sitting in the living room when I walked in, and as usual, she wanted to talk.

"Long day? You look worn out."

"You can't tell?"

"Well, I cooked dinner. I didn't know what time you was coming home, so I didn't warm it up."

"I'm too damn tired to eat. Can you put a cup of soup in the microwave while I shower?"

That night, I ate the cup of soup and jumped into bed. *Sierra is back,* I thought before I dozed off.

Chapter Three

Azir Jackson

Eighteen Years Later . . .

To understand my rage, you must first understand my pain. Shit, I felt like my destiny was carved out from birth.

I've heard plenty of stories about my pops, but I never got the chance to meet him. My grandma often told me stories about how great he was and how much I resembled him. She would smile when she looked at me, saying I reminded her of him. She also kept a picture of him on the dresser, and I could say I do see the resemblance. Fuck that; we looked like twins. The only difference was, he had long hair, and I had dreads.

I spent many days in my backyard wondering if he were here, how much different my life would have been. Now, don't get me wrong, my life wasn't bad at all. Shit, I lived in one of the most exotic countries, Jamaica, that is. I got money at my disposal. My grandma said we weren't rich, but fuck what she was saying. Life was great. We lived in a big-ass mansion up in Beverly Hills. Soon as I got my driver's license, she bought me a Benz. My pocket stayed on swole with U.S. dollars. Mom-dukes also sent me money e'ery month. I haven't seen her in years, but I talked to her on the phone every day.

In my area, people knew me as "Top Shotta." Yeah, they nicknamed me after the movie *Shottas,* only I was the real big man 'round here.

Niggas gave me respect, and the ones that didn't respect were often dealt with. Bitches were all over my dick. Had a few of them tried to put their babies on me, which was definitely a warning; that's why I made sure I wasn't fucking them raw.

I wasn't ready to play daddy; besides, I was getting ready to fly out. I was leaving Jamaica to go live with Mom-dukes. Was ready for the change; plus, I had some serious questions to ask her about Pops, and who killed him. I tried asking Grandma, but her response has always been the same. "Azir baby, God will deal with them."

I understood about her faith, but that wasn't telling me what the fuck happened. There's not one night that I lay in my bed and don't think about the man in the picture. Rage consumes my heart, and my judgment's clouded with anger and hate.

I knew I wouldn't get the answer sitting around in the islands. For the next few months, I worked on my illegal mentality. I prepared myself for the task that was ahead of me. I wasn't sure what he was or who it was against. All I knew was the minute that I touched down in the U.S., I was going to holla at my father's partnas, get a better insight of what the fuck happened to him.

"Yo, Z, I heard yuh 'bout fi leave di place, mi general," Kimari said.

"Yo, Don, dis is mi home, but mi 'ave some things fi handle ova foreign. You see mi?"

"Seen, mi G. Mi only wish me could come wit' yuh."

"Listen, brethren, yuh a mi bredda fi life, and mi know you got me, so just kno' sey yuh bwoy good. Shit real personal wit' me."

"Mi hear you, mi G. Just nuh trust none a dem Yankee bwoy deh. 'Cause fi real, a foreign yuh born, but a yaad you grow up. So yuh a one a we."

"Trust mi, mi dupes, mi nuh trust nuh man. A Jah alone I and I put I trust in. And nuh bloodclaat bwoy can't touch mi. A me name Top Shotta."

Shit, Kimari had been my nigga from day one. We've fucked some of the same bitches, ate out of the same pot, and when it came down to beef, we busted our guns together. Trust me; I loved him like a brother, and I knew he felt the same way. I also knew he was feeling salty that I was leaving.

"Yo, mi G, mi 'bout fi go inna di house. We wi link up early inna di mawning, so we can go up a Papine."

"A'ight, yo."

Pop! Pop! Pop!

"A wey the bomboclaat," I said, as I pulled my gun and fired back at whoever was in a red Toyota Corolla.

Pop! Pop! Pop! More shots were fired as the car circled around and came back toward us.

Even though Kimari and I were shooting back at them niggas, we were no match for the bullets that were coming our way.

"Yo, mek, we mek a run fi it."

We both started busting back while we made our exit. We jumped in my ride, and I sped off down the road. This was my area, so I knew all the back roads; it was nothing to lose those niggas. After I made sure that no one was following us, I pulled into Kimari's driveway. There's no way I was going by my grandma's house 'cause whoever them niggas was, I couldn't risk getting my grandma involved in it.

I was tight as fuck that I didn't get to see their faces. It also bothered me that I didn't know which of them hating-ass niggas was behind the shit.

"Yo, pour mi a shot a rum," I said as I started to roll up a big-head spliff.

"Yo, a who yuh tink dem bwoy is?"

"Bwoy, mi nuh kno'. The first ting cum a mi mind is di bwoy dem from round Matches Lane. Memba di other day mi and di bwoy Markie kick off?"

"Yeah, dem must 'ave a death wish, coming 'round here like that. Di next time mi si dah bwoy, deh is a bullet mi ago put inna him pussyclaat dome. Yuh si mi."

It was kind of a tense ride from the house to the airport. My grandma had tears in her eyes, and earlier before we left, I heard her crying and calling out to God for help. I ain't gonna lie; I was gonna miss her. Shit, she'd been the only person that was constant in my life; no matter what happened or what we went through, she always had my back.

"A'ight, Mama, it's time for me to check in."

"Azir, mi a warn yuh. Nuh badda go gi yuh madda no hard time and stay outta trouble. Foreign nuh nice atall."

"Mama, cho mon. Nuh worry yuhself. Mi good, trust mi; a Jackson mi name, you seet."

She held me for a few more seconds, then let me go. I walked off with my head down. I didn't turn around 'cause I couldn't bear to see the pain she was experiencing. I was also eager to get on the plane and get to Atlanta.

I boarded Delta flight 1877 from Kingston to Hartsfield-Jackson International Airport. As soon as I was seated, I opened my book bag and pulled out the manila envelope that I grabbed from under my grandma's mattress. I wasn't sure what was inside, but I did know that for several years, my grandma would pull it out and sit down reading while she cried. I was never allowed in her room by myself. This morning was different; she asked me to grab her sweater, so I took the opportunity and grabbed the envelope that I knew had something to do with my pops.

I busted the envelope open, and there were newspaper clippings and pictures. I wasted no time; I dug right into the contents of the papers. In front of me were details about what happened to my pops. Water gathered in my eyes as my heart raced. Rage filled my heart. Those fucking pigs shot my pops down as if he were an animal. I fumed as I continued to read every little detail on those pages.

Chapter Four

Sierra Rogers

Today was definitely a day to celebrate. I was on my way to Hartsfield-Jackson to pick up my baby boy. Damn, time flew by so fast; it seemed like it was yesterday he was born, but he was a grown man now, and I haven't seen him in years. I've seen pictures of him, talked to him every day, but by the time I got myself together and was ready to bring him back to the U.S., he was in a good school in Jamaica. His grandmother and I decided it was best he completes high school out there and once he graduates, he would move back to the States.

I still believe in my heart that it was the best move I'd made when I allowed him to stay in Jamaica with his grandma. At first, everything seemed fine . . . right up to the point a few years ago when his grandma called. She informed me that Azir was into the streets, and she had a feeling he was dealing drugs and involved in gang activities.

I froze up on the phone when I heard her utter those words. It brought me back directly to his father. I had hoped that my child wouldn't follow down the same path as his father. It's crazy because he was only weeks old when his father was gunned down. After I got off the phone, I decided to bring him back to the States. The same lifestyle that I was trying to shield him from was the very one he was involved in.

I remembered when I asked him about it, and he flat-out denied that he was in the streets. My mother's intuition kicked in, and I knew then he was lying to me. Azir had no idea how wicked these streets were. I needed him here with me so I could try to keep an eye on him. I refused to lose my baby to these streets.

As I stood waiting for him to come out, I felt butterflies in my stomach. I couldn't wait to snatch him up in my arms. I knew Alijah was staring down at me, smiling. If only he could be here with us.

I recognized him as soon as he hit the corner. He was the dead stamp of his daddy.

"Hey, baby," I screamed and ran over to him.

I grabbed him and hugged him real tight.

"Yo, wha gwaan mi madda," he said in his raw Jamaican accent.

"Boy, if you don't stop sounding like your daddy," I scolded and laughed.

"It's mi swag, Ma, don't be mad at me."

We walked over to the luggage area. I couldn't stop staring at him. Seeing him on Skype and pictures over the years was not the same as seeing him in person. He was taller than me, and it seemed like he'd been working out. He grabbed his luggage off the carousel, and we walked out to my car.

"Damn, Ma, is that you?" He pointed to my Lexus truck.

"Yes, Azir, this me. You may not know it, but your momma likes nice things as well."

"Shit, mi hate that mi affi leave fimi ride."

"Boy, you better watch your mouth." I playfully tried to hit him. "Respect."

His accent was so thick; you couldn't tell this boy was born in Richmond, Virginia, and not Kingston, Jamaica. I swear I understand him a little 'cause I was used to his father's accent, but he needs to speak English 'round here, so I could fully understand.

***

I drove from the airport to Stone Mountain. It's a suburb about thirty minutes out of Atlanta. I had a nice three-bedroom house in the upper-class neighborhood. The entire ride, we talked about his life in Jamaica and his plans for the future.

"So how do you feel, and was your grandma crying?"

"Mi feel good still. Trying to see what America have fi offer. Grandma cool enuh. Dun know, she goin' miss mi still."

"Well, I'm happy you're here now. We don't miss out on so much. We got a lot of catching up to do."

There was a lot of traffic, but we eventually made it home. I know he's probably hungry and tired by now.

"Jeannette, we're here," I yelled as we entered the house.

"It's about time; I've been waiting for y'all. The food must be cold by now," she complained.

"Grandma Jeanette."

"Well, hello, there, young man. C'mon give your nana a big hug."

Azir rushed over and hugged his grandma. They behaved like they didn't want to let go.

"Boy, look at you! You done turned into a man. Last time I seen you, you was a little boy around twelve, I think. Now you all grown up and tall as hell."

"Go upstairs. Your room is still the same way you left it, the last time you visited."

I then walked into the kitchen behind Jeanette. I was starved, and I knew she put her foot in the vegetable stir-fry that she made. I had to give it to her ass; she knew how to throw down in the kitchen.

"Hmm . . . It smell good up in 'ere," Azir said as he walked into the kitchen.

"Yeah, it do. Your grandma is a beast in the kitchen. Go wash yo' hands while I fix yo' plate."

"Oh yes! You kno' mi love fi eat. Anyting except for meat."

"Boy, you missing out on meat. I sure love some oxtail and chicken."

I made plates for the three of us, and we sat down at the dining table. As I sat across from Azir, I couldn't stop admiring him. He was no longer my baby boy; he had turned into a jovial young man. He was tall and muscular. He resembled his father to the teeth. It broke my heart that Alijah wasn't here to see his only seed.

"Yuh good, Mama?"

"Yes, baby. Just looking at how you've grown up."

"Yeah, mon, mi is not a baby anymore," he said.

Azir Jackson

It didn't take me long to fall into my new life in the A. I fit right in with the other Jamaicans, and in no time, I had a little team of yaad boys. I chilled on the low because I was trying to scope out my new surroundings. Late at night, I'd be in my room, writing music and working on my illegal mentality. I was trying to figure out how to flood the area with fresh coke from Jamaica. I had a connect back home but just had to draw up a plan on how to get it into Atlanta. One of the biggest issues I had was trusting these niggas; even though I rolled with them, it didn't mean I trusted them. I was missing my homies back in Jamaica, especially my right-hand man.

It took me awhile to get used to being around Mom, even though she seemed cool. I guess at first, I didn't really give her a chance. Growing up as a child in Jamaica and seeing my homies with their moms and pops, I used to feel some type of way. Pops was dead, but I always wondered why she wasn't there more. I used to come up for summer holidays a few times, but I wanted to live with her. I remember nights lying in bed just thinking about her. My grandma did the best she could, but it wasn't the same; I always felt empty inside. No disrespect, but I turned to the streets because I was searching for the family that I never had. I had some granduncles, but one was a crackhead, and the other always had his hand out every time I went around. It was cool at first, but then I cut that shit off. Fuck them. Ain't shit was wrong with them, so why couldn't they work? I heard stories that my dad used to look out for them. Guess what? I wasn't my dad, and in my book, if a nigga didn't work, then the motherfucka didn't eat.

I heard a loud knock on the door, which immediately interrupted my thoughts.

"Gimme a minute," I hollered after I hid my gun underneath my mattress. "Come on in."

"Hey, baby boy, it's yo' mama," Mom-dukes said as she peeked her head in the door.

"Hey, Ma, wha a gwaan?"

"Nothing much. Just wanted to talk to you 'bout school and your future."

"School? I'm done wit' that."

"Done? You're only finished wit' high school. Now you need to get into college so that you can get an education."

"Listen, Ma, no disrespect to you, but a my music mi a pursue right yah now."

"Music? You need a freaking education first; then you can talk 'bout music."

"Nah, that's wha *you* want. A nuh dat mi a pree."

"Boy, listen, you came here to go to school and get yo' life in order. I be damn if I'm going to sit around and watch you waste your life. Don't think your grandma didn't tell me 'bout you running the streets."

"Like mi tell yuh before, I 'ont know what she told you, but fi real, I wasn't doing shit."

"Boy, you better watch yo' mouth. I know one thing; as long as you live under my roof, you will get a job or go to school."

"Ma, a nuh nothin' to move out. Just cum out an sey it."

"You missing the point. I lost yo' daddy to the streets, and there's no way I'm going to lose my only child too. The streets don't love nobody, and these niggas you're running with are the same ones that will turn on you. You better listen."

"So let me get dis right . . . 'cause Pops messed up his life, so mi affi suffer fi dat? I'm not 'im; I wish you realize dat. All mi life, all mi hear is Alijah this, Alijah dat. Goddamn, mi is not Alijah.

Mi a Azir. Go off on me when mi mess up, not off what Alijah did wit' fi 'im life."

I swear I was sick and tired of all these mutha-fuckers using my pop's shit to throw at me. The fucked-up part is they were not telling the entire story.

"Azir, baby, I know I haven't been there like I was supposed to, but I was going through a rough time after your dad passed and me getting shot. I thought leaving you with your grandma was the best thing to do for you." Tears started to flow down my face.

"Ma, come here. Don't do dat. You know mi hate fi see yuh cry. I didn't mean fi get yuh upset." I got up and wrapped my arms around her.

"Ma, mi know yuh love mi and want di best fi mi, but me is no longer a little yute. Mi is a grown man now, and mi 'ave to mek mi own mistake dem."

I knew she was hurting, but I had to keep it one hunnit wit' her. I wasn't going to college, and I wasn't gonna lie to make her happy. Hustling was in my blood, and there was no way I was leaving the streets; not now, anyway. Things were finally coming together; I'd linked up with some cats, and we were getting ready to show these li'l hustlers in the A how it's really done. Top Shotta Posse was getting ready to take over.

She finally got her tears under control. I took her hands and looked her in the eyes.

"Aye, Ma, I'm not a little boy no mo'. I want to know what went down with my pops, you, and that other woman."

"Azir, what other woman are you talking 'bout?"

"Ma, come on. That Shayna lady, Pop's wife."

I peeped the surprise on her face. Yeah, I read all that in the papers that my grandma was hiding. I was tired of e'erybody trying to lie to me. Shit, I was grown; trust me, I could handle the truth.

We sat on the bed together as she took me on a journey of when she and Pops met, along with details about e'erything that went down between them. This was the first time I was getting a clear picture of how important my dad was. I was shocked to know he was a kingpin. By the time she got to the part about getting shot, my blood was boiling. I continued listening so I could get an understanding of how things played out. I felt a tear drop on my arm. This bitch name Shayna not only tried to kill my mom twice, she even threatened *my* life, set my dad up with the feds, and she was still breathing. I had a few questions, but the main one was, if my pops was such a thoroughbred, why didn't he body this

bitch when he first learned that she was fuckin'
his homeboy? This was one of the reasons why I
didn't trust them bitches. They ain't loyal.

"Ma, mi about to head to Atlanta." I kissed her
on the forehead.

"Please be careful out there in them streets."
She grabbed my arm.

"Ma, trust me, mi careful." I smiled and walked
off.

I couldn't wait to get out of the crib. I locked
the front door and jumped into my ride. I pulled
a bag of Dro out of my glove compartment and
rolled it up. I sat in the driveway and took a few
pulls. The minute the ganja hit my brain, it was
like it gave me a new life. I no longer felt closed
in.

As I pulled off, I noticed Mom-dukes peeping
out of her bedroom window. I wish she'd lighten
up a little. After our talk tonight, I had a better
understanding, and I could respect her feelings
more. It placed a smile on my face, knowing I
came from the strong love that they shared. It
sounded like the perfect hood story with an
unhappy ending.

Driving down I-20 heading toward Atlanta,
all kinds of evil thoughts invaded my mind. That
bitch Shayna fucked up my family over some
paper. This bitch had to pay for her actions. As

a young yute, I vowed to get at whoever crossed my pops. I'd always thought it was a dude, only to find out it was the bitch he married. I didn't know how it was going down, because the bitch was in prison. I had to think clearly because one false move could seal my fate. Jah knows I couldn't continue living my life as if nothing happened. *The bitch has to be stopped,* I thought.

Chapter Five

Shayna Jackson

"Ha-ha," I busted out laughing while I lay on my bunk. I thought I couldn't survive one day in prison, but here I was, still breathing. I'd just finished my eighteenth year. I done changed prisons twice, and now I was in Tallahassee FCI. It's funny how the feds lock you up in one state, then ship your ass all the way over to the other side of the country.

I lay on the bed contemplating my next move. I damn sure was tired of these lower-class bitches and these fucking guards trying to ruin my life. I mostly hang out at the law library reading up on different cases, or sometimes I might help some of these bitches write up appeal letters. This shit wasn't free, so best believe that their family members were putting that money into my account.

It was during one of my researches that my next grand plan slipped in my mind. I almost started laughing, but I looked around and noticed all the nosy bitches were present. I gathered my things and quietly exited the library. A plan like this needed a lot of thorough thinking and had to be executed at the appropriate time.

See, in female prisons, the guards are usually overfriendly, especially if you are a pretty inmate. I've had quite a few of them flirt with me or say little nasty things to me. I usually dismiss that shit. I was well aware they were only trying to fuck. Only this time, I had a plan, and this one officer was going to be part of my plan.

I jumped off my bunk, straightened my gray sweatpants, and sashayed up to the front office.

"Hey, Officer Gonzalez. How you doing today?" I said in my sexy voice.

"Well, hello, there, Jackson. I'm doing better now that I've laid eyes on a beautiful sister like you."

"I'm happy that I could make you feel better," I replied as I licked my finger and pointed it at him.

"Jackson, you really shouldn't play wit' my emotions like that," he grinned.

I glanced at the nosy bitch from D.C. as she walked by; she was trying her best to eavesdrop on our conversation.

"Thanks for the advice," I said. Once she was gone, I turned my full attention back to Gonzalez. "Who said I was playing? I see how you look at me with lust in your eyes. Trust me; I know you want some of this high-grade pussy. I haven't met a nigga yet that could resist this." I pointed down to my crotch.

"You're one beautiful woman. I can't help it."

"Well, what are we going to do about it, then?"

"Is that an invitation, Jackson?"

"Unless you're too scared to be with a *real* woman," I teased.

"Ha-ha. Me scared? Never."

"Well, prove it, then," I said while staring at his cock, which, by the way, was bulging out of his uniform pants.

After a few days of us playing around with each other, we finally decided to do something about it. I was ready, and I could tell he was also ready to devour this pussy.

It was a little past 11:00 p.m. I lay on my bunk staring at the ceiling, waiting until after count was done, and the lights were turned off. Then

I got off my bunk and grabbed a glove that I got earlier. I stuffed it in my pants pocket; then I walked toward the shower room, which was closed for the night. I got into the last booth, farthest away from the door. There I took off my pajama pants and my underwear. Shit, I was excited that I was about to get fucked. It's been years since I've felt a cock inside of me. I was kind of nervous, but fuck it; I was *that* bitch. I watched as he stepped into the booth that could barely hold both of us.

He wasted no time; he started to fondle me. I wasn't going to lie; the touch of his hand on my pussy sent an electrifying feeling through my entire body. I knew we were pressed for time before another guard entered the unit. I immediately unzipped his pants and took his over-sized cock out of his briefs. I turned away from him so that he could slide inside of me from the back.

He started penetrating me hard; I was under extreme pressure. Maybe it was the fact that my pussy hadn't gotten fucked in a while. He grabbed me by the back of my neck as he applied more pressure. I tried not to lose focus on why I was in the damn shower fucking this nigga in the first place.

"Babe, this pussy is so damn good," he whispered in my ear.

"Let me suck you off, daddy."

He slid his cock out, and I got on my knees. I slowly licked my pussy juice off his cock. I then devoured his thick, oversized, Puerto Rican cock in my mouth. He grabbed my neck and tried to ram the whole thing down my throat. Any other time I'd have snapped; instead, this time, I welcomed his aggressiveness.

"Oh shit, mami, I'm about to come," he barely whispered.

That was my cue to suck harder on his cock. I locked my mouth down on that cock and sucked it like my life depended on it, which, in reality, it really did.

"Oh oh oh," he said before he let out his cock juice into my mouth.

I quickly got up, turned around away from him, pretending as if I was gathering my clothes. In fact, I had other things in mind.

I watched as he tucked his cock back into his pants, pulled the curtain, and disappeared into the dark hallway. I tied up the glove and put my clothes on, peeped to see if the coast was clear, which it was, then I walked back to my living area, put the gloves inside of my locker, and grabbed my mouthwash. I walked to the sink and rinsed my mouth out twice.

After that, I walked back quietly, locked my locker, and got into my bed. I was careful not to wake up my bunkie; that nosy bitch that couldn't hold water. I watched as Officer Gonzalez walked back into the office and closed the door. Then I put my headphones on, thinking of what to do next.

I got up bright and early, feeling like a brand-new woman with a better outlook on life. I had my counseling session with Doctor Carr. See, this stupid-ass judge decided that after all this shit that happened, I needed mental health counseling. I know I wasn't fucking crazy or have I ever pretended like I was crazy. I have to admit, though, I love going to these little sessions to toy around with Doctor Carr's feelings. Today was different, though, Doctor Carr was going to help me set this plan into motion. I had one of the best roles in my life coming up, and I had to be mentally prepared.

"Miss Jackson, how are you feeling today?" Doctor Carr asked.

"Not feeling well, but I'm hanging in there," I said, then sat down.

"Sorry to hear that. We can talk about what you're feeling and try to see if we can make you feel a little better."

"Okay." I was preparing myself for the grand moment.

We talked about everything, even about my daddy and me. Doc tried to convince me that Daddy took advantage of me. Fuck what he was saying. Daddy and I had a special bond. I remember the first time Daddy touched my breast; it was special. I felt love, and as time went by, I fell deeper in love with him. He gave me all the attention that I needed. I started to hate Mama; I wished she would move away so Daddy and I could live happily together.

"Shayna." This fool interrupted my good thoughts.

"Yes, sorry. I was in another zone," I replied with a sad look plastered across my face.

"What's bothering you today? You seem to have something heavy on your mind."

I busted out crying.

"I'm sorry! Did I say something wrong?"

Poor old fool, he's just like a man, I thought.

"No, no. It's just that I don't want to get anyone in trouble."

"Get who in trouble? Your dad is dead, so it's too late to prosecute him."

"No, not Daddy . . ." I managed to get out, while my crying got louder.

"Shayna, I'm all ears. Who is this person, and what kind of trouble are you referring to?"

"If you insist, but you cannot tell this to anyone, Doc. Officer Gonzalez has been forcing me to have sex with him."

"Officer Gonzalez? Is that an officer here at the prison?" He looked puzzled.

"Yes, he works the night shift."

"Oh, my. How long has this been going on?"

"Around three weeks," I mumbled.

"Can you tell me about it?" He reached over and took ahold of my hands.

"He told me if I didn't have sex with him, he would get me in big trouble."

"Do you know what kind of trouble he was referring to?"

"No. I wasn't sure. But I've heard many stories about officers planting evidence or throwing inmates in lockup for months when they deny sexual advances."

I went on to tell him what I needed him to know about what went down between Gonzalez and me. I made sure I emphasized I was an unwilling recipient in this shit.

"I do not doubt you, but do you have any evidence of what you told me?"

"No, I can't . . . I-I don't want to get him in any trouble; plus, he said if I told anyone, they're not going to believe me, and I'll end up doing more time. I don't want to risk getting life in prison."

"Shayna, you're a victim of sexual assault. He used his power to engage you in sexual activities. It's considered rape because you're a federal inmate, and he's an officer. He abused his power, and this needs to be reported."

I started to bawl harder and louder. That was *exactly* what I needed to hear. Someone that actually believed me and my lies.

"I know this is hurtful, but do you mind if I share this with the lieutenant? He needs to be punished for what he did. It is confidential when you confide in me, but I can share this with your permission. If you don't want me to, I understand."

"No, I give you my permission. I'm just tired and want it to go away."

I watched as he walked out the door, and within five minutes, he returned with Lieutenant Fernandez.

Here we go, I thought.

"Miss Jackson, please tell the lieutenant what you told me."

I turned around to face the lieutenant. I made sure he could see the pain I was experiencing. I told my story to the very attentive lieutenant. After I finished talking, she accompanied me to my locker to retrieve the glove that I had spit his come in.

I also made a written statement. After they left, some of the nosy bitches came over to ask me what was going on. I rolled my eyes and walked off. These bitches were not going to fuck up what I had going on. I walked into the phone booth and dialed my lawyer's number. I wasn't a fool; I was well aware that all phone calls were recorded. I told my lawyer about the rape that took place and let him know there was an active case going on. I made sure to let him know I was scared for my life, and I was fearful I might become a target of this officer's revenge. I needed my lawyer to call the prison and get all the details concerning this case. I was ready to get the fuck up out of here.

Azir Jackson

It took me about a year to build a solid empire and make a name for myself in the drug world. Soon as my name started popping, I started to feel the heat from the down South niggas. The niggas were trying their hardest to make us acknowledge them, but we were not trying to fuck with no outside niggas. The fact was they didn't like outsiders coming in their state and selling shit. They had a bigger problem when it came down to us Jamaicans.

My entire crew was made up of Kingston cats. Jah T was from Seaview Gardens, Corey and Trevor were from Cockburn Pen. These cats were official top shottas that were willing to bust their guns in a quick second. A few times, I had to tell my niggas to back down, 'cause they were ready to go to war with these Yankee niggas. I learned early on that you can't beef and make money. Don't get me wrong; if a nigga violate, he *will* be dealt with, but that unnecessary beef was in the way of stacking paper.

We didn't hustle dime bags; we got right into dealing with kilos of pure white fresh off the boat, getting it into our warehouse that we had out in Norcross.

I was so caught up in the streets that I almost forgot that I had serious business to tend to. It was time to get my plan in motion. I searched and found a PI. I called him, and we decided to meet up.

I saw the Jeep Cherokee that he described to me parked on the side of Wade Walker's Park. I pulled my truck as close as I could get; then I exited the vehicle and walked closer toward him.

"Mr. Salmon, I'm Abe, nice to meet you."

"Whaddup?" I gave him dap.

"Okay, so you have a job for me? Spit it out."

"I'ma need to know that I can trust you with what I'm about to ask you to do."

"Of course. I ain't been in this business over thirty-something years by running my mouth," he chuckled.

"A'ight, cool. Listen, this woman in this picture is very special to me, but I lost contact with her. I need you to find her, and I need to know everything that she's been up to."

"She's pretty. Must be very special."

"You have no idea." I shot him a fake grin.

I handed him ten grand and walked off. I jumped into my ride and cut up the music. Sizzla's "Just One of Those Days" blasted through my speakers as I drove down Rockbridge Road. I was headed to this bitch's house that I was fucking. I was in a good mood and needed some pussy to finish the day off right.

My phone started to ring. I looked down at the caller ID and saw it was my favorite lady.

"Hey, beautiful."

"Hey, baby boy. I haven't seen or heard from you since yesterday," she fussed.

"I know, been busy dealing wit' some tings."

"Busy? Azir, you don't have no damn job, so what you busy doing?"

"C'mon, Ma. Mi wi si yuh lata."

Dang! Mom-dukes be ridin' the fuck outta me, I thought as I took a few pulls out of the blunt. She needs to lighten up a little.

I pulled up at shorty's house and made sure I parked in the back. Didn't like my ride to be too visible. I locked my ride, walked up the stairs, and knocked on the door.

"Who is it?"

"Girl, you better stop playin'."

She opened the door, looking radiant as usual, except for the attitude on her face. I walked past her and headed to the living room.

"I've been calling you for days. You 'ont pick up yo' phone, but here you are popping up and shit."

"Yo, B, I been busy. I told you when I'm in the streets so it hard fi focus pon personal shit."

"Boy, whatever! You ain't working twenty-four hours a day. I'm not goin' keep being ya fool. The only time I see you is when you want pussy."

"Ma, go ahead wit' all that. I a man, get pussy pon the regular, so it can't be dat. Mi really like yuh."

"Oh, when I met you, you claimed you didn't have anyone, but now you claiming you get pussy on the regular. You are a fucking liar and a cheater."

"Yo, shut up! I ain't come over here fo' all that. Come ride this dick fo' me."

"Nah, fuck you. You betta call one of them bitches you be fucking. I'm good."

"That's how you feel? Cool, I'm out." I got up to leave.

She jumped in front of me and put her hand on my chest to ease me back. "So you just goin' leave like that?"

"Quit playing wit' me. Mi like yuh, but mi can't tek all dis bitching. Shut the fuck up sometimes; maybe den, a nigga will come around mo'."

"You ain't got to keep talking crazy to me." She shoved me.

"Come here, girl." I snatched her little ass up.

I put her down on the couch and slid off the little dress that she was wearing. To my surprise, shorty didn't have on any drawers. This bitch had a badass body, firm breasts, and a fat pussy.

"Come here, mon." I pulled her head down to my waist.

She knew what time it was, 'cause she took my dick out and immediately went to work. The head was like that, and I felt the urge to come, but I held back. When I couldn't take it anymore, I pulled her up, turned her around, and slid my dick into her slippery pussy.

"Aargh, aargh," I growled as I entered her.

"Baby, take your time," she begged.

"Man, yo' pussy too fucking good. I can't take mi time." I thrust my dick deep up in the hole that had a tight grip on my dick. It didn't take long for me to bust all up inside of her.

"Fuck!" I yelled.

"Damn, you just bust in me."

"Man, I fucked up! Tell me yuh deh pon di pill!"

"Hell no! I ain't on no pill!"

"Well, I smoke too much ganja; my sperm count is weak."

"It better be, 'cause I'm not ready for no baby. I got three more years of college to go."

"I feel you on that."

I swear my ass whispered a silent prayer to Jah. I wasn't ready to be no daddy. Besides, I didn't want my seed to go through the things that I went through—no mom or pops around.

I went into the bathroom to clean myself off. While in there I heard shorty on the phone, but I couldn't hear what she was saying. *Shit, she must be bragging about this dick whipping she got,* I thought and smiled.

I got dressed and kissed her on the forehead. I was 'bout to bounce.

"Damn, nigga, all you do is come fuck and leave."

"Yo, I got moves to make. I'll be back later, ma."

"Whatever; one of these fucking days, I ain't go be here when you come knocking."

"Girl, yo' ass ain't nowhere. You know you love this dick," I joked.

"Keep thinking that shit," she said before she slammed the door in my face.

Her ass is tripping, I thought as I walked down the stairs. I looked down for a quick second as I fumbled around in my pocket, trying to retrieve my keys.

"Nigga, don't move," a dude's voice said as he stuck a pistol in my back.

"I ain't moving my nigga."

I was caught slipping. I knew it was too late to grab my burner off my waist.

"Lemme get this off you." He took my gun off my waist.

I stood there thinking about going at this nigga, but he had his gun aimed at me, and I didn't want to risk getting shot.

"Yo, partna, empty yo' pockets and let's take a li'l walk over to yo' ride."

"Fo' what? Ain't shit in my ride, but dig into my pocket. I got a stack."

"Nah, fuck that. Let's go, or I'll splatter your fucking brains all over the sidewalk."

"A'ight, brethren. I'm parked in the back."

My mind was racing. I had no idea what the plan was—I didn't know if the nigga was tryin'a kill me. I walked toward my ride, with this bitch-ass nigga right behind me. His gun was still poking me in the back.

"Yo, brethren, what's yo' beef wit' me?"

"Ain't no beef, partna. Do what I ask, and e'erything will be cool. You feel me? Lemme get them keys."

The nigga got in my face, but what surprised me was this fool wasn't wearing a mask. I recognized his face from somewhere. Just wasn't sure where.

"Damn, partna, I thought you ain't had nothin' in here. Look what I found."

My heart sank because I already knew what was in there; it was some work and 'bout ten stacks that I was supposed to drop off.

He grabbed the work and the money and threw my keys on the ground. A car pulled up, and he took off running with my burner and jumped into the car.

I picked up my keys and jumped in my ride. My first instinct was to follow them, but it was useless. I didn't have no heat on me. I dialed Jah T's number.

"Yo, wha gwaan mi linky?"

"Yo, you won't believe this. I just got robbed!"

"Wha di bloodclaat yuh a sey?" he yelled.

"Yo, mi was leaving outta di Yankee gyal down on Rockbridge house, and a bwoy creep up behind me and stick him gun inna mi back."

"Man, wha the fuck? Did yuh si di bwoy face? Dat pussyhole dead."

"Yo, mi see the bwoy face somewhere before. Just can't remember weh."

"Well, fuck it. Yuh already know wey we need fi do."

"No doubt! I'ma leave from 'round here. Where yuh at?"

"At the spot. I'ma call the other fellas."

"Bet. Mi on di way."

"A'ight. One."

I turned on my truck and pulled off, but before I exited the subdivision, I looked up and saw that bitch peeping through her blinds. I could've sworn I peeped a smirk on her face. I kept on going, but I made a mental note to follow up on that.

By the time I got to N. Hairston, all my niggas were present at the stash house.

"Yo, whaa agwaan mi dupes?" I gave them daps.

"Yo, mi just hear wha gwaan. You good, fam?" Trevor asked.

"Man, still a breathe, you simmi. Trust mi, di bwoy ketch mi a slip. I was too late to grab my burner. Dawg, I fucked up."

"What I don't get is how dis nigga know to get at you? I think it's that bitch."

"Yuh know what? A di same ting I was thinking about on mi way ova ya. I heard the bitch pon di phone when I went to piss, but by the time mi cum out, she hang up. Didn't tink nothin' 'bout it 'til now."

"The bitch set yuh up, plain and simple."

I'd already thought about that, but to hear those words from my niggas only confirmed it for me. I wondered how stupid this bitch could be. She knew she could get anything from me; it wasn't nothing for me to drop a couple of stacks on her. This bitch done fucked up!

"Yo, roll up a blunt."

"Yo, son, I told you before, these hoes are worse than the ones back home. These bitches ain't loyal. It could've been worse; you could've lost yo' life behind some pussy. You gots to be mo' careful."

"I feel you, but that nigga chose the wrong vic. Trust mi, he's a walking dead right 'bout now." I took a long pull of the ganja and closed my eyes as it hit my brain.

"A'ight, so fuck all that. Bottom line is that bitch set you up. She and that nigga got to be dealt with. Can't let this slide, 'cause that's opening up room for other lame-ass niggas to get at us."

"I feel you, brethren. These niggas will learn."

We continued drinking, chasing blunts after blunts, and discussing business. I was tryin'a decide how to break the news to them that I was gonna be out soon.

"Yo, brethren, mi 'ave a rough day still so mi 'bout to head to Mom-dukes. I'll get up wit' y'all niggas in the a.m."

"Stay up, son," Jah T said.

I walked out the door and jumped in my ride, heading for home. I was tired as fuck and needed to take a shower. I ain't goin' lie; going home was overbearing at times. Mom-dukes stayed riding me about shit. *I hope she ain't home* I thought as I opened the front door.

I walked in, took my shoes off, and headed straight for the stairs.

"Azir, is that you?" Jeanette's voice startled me.

So much for coming home and heading straight to the shower.

"Yeah, Nana. It's me."

"Boy, you had me and yo' mother worried to death."

"Nana, y'all worry too much." I turned around and walked toward the living room.

"Foolishness! There's no such thing as worrying too much. These streets are deadly."

"Tell me about it," I replied and sighed.

"Sit down. I made some tuna salad."

"Nana, I'm beat. I'm 'bout to head upstairs."

"Azir, sit down," she sternly said.

"A'ight, chill out, woman."

I knew some shit was about to be said. I sat beside her on the couch.

"You know I'm the last person to get into yo' business, but you in the streets and heading down the wrong road. You ain't fooling me. I know what you doing out there. You leave out and gone for days, no sleep, come in here with the same outfit on for days. Trust me; I done messed around with a few hustlers back in my day, so I know one when I see one." She looked me dead in the eyes.

"Ha-ha, Nana, you trippin'."

"Nah, I'm not. I know you grown and all, but think about what can happen in those streets and how it's gonna tear yo' mother apart. She already broken from losing yo' daddy. Don't let her lose her only child too," she pleaded while tears flowed from her eyes.

"Nana, chill out. I'm not in the street like that, so you and Ma ain't got nothing to worry 'bout."

"Azir, I've been on this earth way longer than you. I've seen too many deaths, too many mothers holding their stomachs and crying over the loss of their child. You are way too smart for this. Yo' father lost his life to those same streets. Take heed."

"Nana, trust me; I've heard these stories about Pops since I was a little yute, but the truth is, the streets didn't kill Pops. The police killed him." I got up and walked away.

"Owee," I said as I flopped down on my bed.

I missed lying in bed 'cause lately, I've been going so hard at the grind I barely have time to sleep. Whenever I come to Mom-duke's crib, it's time for me to relax and enjoy my nana's cooking. Check this, Pops left me enough paper to last a lifetime, but I wanted my own, from my own sweat. Plus, that was chump change compared to the amount of money I wanted to make. I want to say I made this shit on my own in the end . . .

After the incident earlier, I definitely needed to be more on point. I could've lost my life. I couldn't afford that. I had too much left to do in this fucked-up world, I thought before I dozed off.

Chapter Six

Azir Jackson

I was up at the crack of dawn. Fuck sleeping. I could do that when I'm dead. I got dressed because I had an early-morning meeting with the PI. He sounded eager to help, so let's see what he's got for me.

It's been weeks; I was itching to hear some good news. The closer I got to our meeting spot, the more nervous I started to feel. Man, what the fuck? I've waited for this my entire life, and I was seconds away from getting the info. I pulled my ride close to where he was parked. I got out and walked hurriedly over to him; then I got in the truck with him.

"Whaddup, my man?" I gave him dap.

"Mr. Salmon, how you doing?"

I almost asked who the fuck Mr. Salmon was but quickly caught myself. I'd given him that name when we first spoke on the phone. I had to make sure I didn't slip up in any way.

"I'm good. I see you smilin' and shit, so I take it you got something good fo' me."

"Of course. I think we hit the lottery. Not only did I find your lady friend, but I also found her old bunk mate."

The anticipation was killing me. "Spit it out rude, bwoy."

He went on to give me all the info that I needed and some extra. He found out that her homegirl was right here in Atlanta. This woman was gonna be my number one focus until my goal was accomplished.

"Good looking out, bro. I 'preciate you," I said before I dropped ten stacks on his car seat.

I watched as his eyes lit up.

"Brother, man, thank you. If you ever need anything, don't hesitate to call me."

"Yeah, fo' sho, and, yeah, I do need one thing."

"What's that? Name it; you got it."

"Your complete silence."

"You got it. My lips are sealed."

"Yeah, I know." I pulled out my Glock and shot him in the head.

"Now I know fo' sho," I mumbled to myself.

I snatched the money off the seat and glanced around to make sure no one was in sight. The coast was clear, so I jumped out of his ride and dashed to my truck and slowly pulled out from behind the abandoned building on Walker Road. I looked down at my clothes to make sure there was no evidence of blood. I had on a black shirt, so there wasn't anything visible. I then lit up a blunt and took a few pulls. My phone started ringing. I looked down to see it was the one bitch that I didn't want to hear from.

"Yo!"

"That's how you answer the phone?"

"No, B! But I'm in the middle of something."

"I haven't heard anything from you since you came over and fucked me."

"Yeah, like I said before, I'm in the middle of doing shit. I'll be through there to holla at you later." I hung up the phone before she could say another word.

My anger skyrocketed at the sound of that bitch's voice. I ain't forgot 'bout her ass setting me up. I was tryin'a get shit in order. I didn't want to rush and make a move that could get me killed or locked up.

I found the chick named Natasha, using the info that ole dude gave me. Shit, I found her right on Facebook. I didn't even do that social media shit, but this was necessary. The bitch must have been hard up for dick 'cause soon after I friended her, we started kicking it in the inbox. I expressed to her that I liked her and would love to meet her. Without hesitation, she invited me to her crib.

I got me a rental from one of my links. I couldn't risk getting caught up in my vehicle. This bitch stayed on the west side on Campbellton Road. This was a known drug and homicide area. I done heard some stories from my homies, so I usually stayed away from that area.

I pulled up at the house on the corner. The building looked abandoned. I wasn't feeling it, but I had no choice. I took my burner out of the glove compartment and made sure I had a full clip. I also took out an extra clip and slipped it into my pocket. I stuck my gun in my waist and got out of the car. I dialed her number as I walked toward the house.

"Hello."

"I'm outside. You not goin' let me in?"

"Sure, I'm coming right now."

She must've run to the door because it popped open within seconds.

"Hey, there, Lonzo. Come on in."

"Whaddup, ma?" I had to bring myself to say that shit. The bitch reminded me of the chick that played in the movie *Precious*.

I stepped inside the house and looked around to peep out my environment.

"Sit down. I'm happy that I finally get a chance to meet you," she smiled.

"You have no idea. The feeling is mutual."

"Yeah, I usually don't do this, but I swear I'm feeling you. I've never felt like this over no dude that I've never met before."

"I understand. Come on over here and show me some love."

I stood up, unbuckled my belt, and pulled my pants and boxers down. All that was left was my wood hanging.

"Damn! I th-th-thought . . ." she stuttered.

"I mean we grown; we're into each other, so why not?" I ain't goin' lie. I didn't want to fuck her fat, ugly ass, but I knew to get her where I wanted her, I had to do something; I settled with the head.

"I know. I just didn't want you to think I was no freak."

"Shit, I ain't no li'l boy. Fuck all that. C'mon gi mi some a dat bomb head you be talkin' 'bout." Before I could finish my sentence, shorty was already on her knees.

I had no idea how her big ass got down there that fast. Within seconds, her ass was devouring my wood. She sucked it like she ain't ate in weeks. I ain't goin' front; it felt good as fuck, especially when she deep-throated it. I ain't never met a bitch before that could take all of my wood in her mouth. I bust in no time. Yeah, I ain't pull out. Instead, I let all my seed flow out down her throat. She swallowed every last drop and cleaned my wood off with her tongue.

"Damn, shorty, you a beast."

"Shit, I might not know how to do anything else, but I know how to suck a good dick. Trust that."

"I hear you, ma. Where's the bathroom?"

"The first door on the left."

I cleaned myself off and washed my hands. That was some fire head I thought as I walked back into the living room.

"I cooked. Do you want something to eat?"

"No, I'm good, but I need to holla at you 'bout some serious shit."

"Me? What did I do? It wasn't me," she laughed.

"Nah, sit down, ma. I got a business proposition for you."

"You know I'm scared straight. If it involve breaking the law, I ain't wit' it."

"I ain't asking you to break no law, but it involves ten stacks."

"Ten what?" Her eyes got bigger, and she sat her fat ass down.

"Yeah, I knew this would grab yo' attention. You was at the prison in Tallahassee?"

"Yes, that's where I did my time. How did you know that?"

"That's minor. I got connects."

"I see. So what that got to do with what you need me to do?" she said, looking at me.

"There was a chick there by the name of Shayna Jackson. You two might have been friends."

"Shayna Jackson. Shayna, yeah, I believe if that's the right Shayna, we were bunkies. What about her?"

"Well, I need to get in contact with her, and I need your help."

"Why do you need my help? This don't sound too good."

"Listen, yo, di gyal do some fucked-up shit, and I just need to find her."

She sat there staring at me. I started rubbing on her thighs. She wasn't no dime piece, but I needed her, so I don't mind stroking her ego. She looked at me and smiled.

"I didn't really like the bitch anyway, so I'm sure we can work something out," she smiled and winked at me.

"Listen, here go ten stacks. I know you can use the money."

"Are you serious? What the hell that bitch done did? 'Cause you coming off some stacks."

"There's more where this came from if you keep yo' mouth shut and play yo' position. Trust me; daddy will make sure you a'ight, you hear me?" I said as I threw the cash into her lap.

She looked down at the burner on my hip, then back at me.

"Trust me, I fully understand. You ain't got to worry about me saying a damn word to anyone."

"That's my girl. Now be ready for when she do call. I 'ont want no mess up," I said, while I rubbed her face.

I stayed a few more minutes, explaining everything to her, then I bounced up out of that area. I was heading home, but first I stopped at Family Dollar and bought me a notepad and pen. I had a letter to write to a very special *bitch*. I was a street nigga, but I was good with words, especially when my livelihood depended on it!

After I left shorty's house, I was feeling much better. I could see things were falling into place. I just hope it continues to flow right. I cut the radio on just in time to hear a V103's news reporter saying, "*The body of prominent private investigator Abe Murray was found on the city's east end.*" She went on to say he was killed execution style. The family was offering a reward for the person or persons responsible for this horrible crime. I cut that shit off as I replayed everything in my mind. Earlier, I'd smashed up the prepaid phone that I used to contact him. I gave him a wrong name, so I wasn't worried about that. I was careful in speaking in my best American accent when I dealt with him.

It didn't surprise me how killing had become second nature to me. Growing up in Jamaica and hanging around some of the most ruthless gangstas, I caught on pretty fast. Shit, after all the stories I heard about Pops, I'm surprised that motherfuckas expect different from me. Well, in a way, I was different. He was too trusting of motherfuckas. Not I. In my world, e'erybody suspect, even Mom-dukes. Shit, I feel like if the right pressure is applied, she'll crack. That's why when I do my dirt, I do it alone. Don't get me wrong; I fuck with my niggas, but certain shit I keep to myself, 'cause I ain't tryin'a spend the rest of my life in nobody cell. You feel me? Shit, I love money and pussy too much.

Driving through the city, I noticed DeKalb pigs were out in full force. I decided to call it a night, so I went in the house early. I felt the same feelings that I felt e'erytime I entered the house. It was time to get my own crib.

I heard the living room television come on, so I peeped my head in. I noticed Mom-dukes watching the news. *Dang, this lady stays watching the news,* I thought.

"That's you, Azir?" she hollered.

"Yeah, Ma." I walked over to her and planted a big kiss on her cheeks.

"Sit down." She patted the couch.

Oh, here we go again, I thought.

"What's good, Ma? You a'ight?"

"Yeah, I'm good. The question is, what's going on with my son?"

"Ain't nothing going on. I'm chilling."

"Azir, I watch you come and go. I know what you're in these streets doing. I went into your room to clean it the other day, and you know what I found? These." She showed me my baby 9 mm and 'bout an ounce of powder.

"Man, why were you in my room snooping in the first place?" I looked at her.

"Snooping? Boy, you done lost yo' damn mind. This is *my* house, and you 'ont pay no damn bills in here," she said in a fierce tone.

"I know it's your house and shit, but I'm a grown man, and you in my room going through my stuff."

"Azir, you listen up good. This shit should never be in my house. You're out there breaking the law, and there is only one of two outcomes. Either you goin' get killed, or yo' ass gonna be locked up in jail like an animal. Alijah is turning over in his grave right now at your actions. Your daddy busted his ass to make sure you ain't want for nothing. Your ass not in these streets because you're poor; yo' ass is out there 'cause you want to be. It's not because you hungry or homeless. Wake up, Azir. Take some of that money and go to college. Get a career; make something of yourself."

"Dang, Ma. A whole speech, though? I'm not you or Pops. It's my life, and I'm goin' live it."

"You know what? Yes, it's your life, but as long as you live under *my* roof, it's *my* rules. I'm not goin' be no part of you messing up yo' life."

"You know what? I see that I can never live up to your expectations. I'm not Alijah; stop expecting me to mess up just 'cause he did. You know you so hard on me, but you was his side woman and supported everything he did. I'm your son. Why can't I get yo' support for once?"

"Boy, shut the fuck up talking 'bout things you know nothing about. I wasn't side to anyone. I *was* his woman; he came home to me. He loved me. Don't you ever turn your mouth to even disrespect me like that anymore," she yelled and got up and walked away.

The second those words left my mouth, I regretted it. I love Mom-dukes, and honestly, I know that she loves me. It's just that sometimes, it's too much. *"Alijah this, Alijah that."* I was sick of that shit. Guess what? Alijah been dead and ain't coming back. She needed to get over it and move on. Dang, she just blew my mood. I turned around and went back out the door. I jumped in my car and headed for Memorial Drive. I stopped at the liquor store, got me a bottle of gin and some blunts, and then I got me a room at Quality Inn on Memorial. I needed some time alone to get my thoughts together and focus on what's important to me.

I took a quick shower, rolled a big head, and took the bottle of gin to the head. Then I sat in the dark, zoned out, thinking of my life, the past, and the present. I felt a few teardrops falling; no one understood the pain I was feeling inside. Ever since I was a little yute, I've always had this emptiness deep down. It ain't about no money or how much shit I had. Don't none of that matter.

What matters to me was me getting revenge on the muthafucka that fucked my life up and took my pops away.

I cut the light on and grabbed my notepad. I had a letter to write to a very special lady.

Shayna Jackson.

Hey, the Beautiful Miss Jackson,

I hope this letter finds you in the best of health. I know you're wondering who this is, so let me introduce myself. My name is Alonzo Caldwell. I'm the first cousin of your ex-bunkie Natasha Caldwell. She left the facility 'bout a year and a half ago. Anyway, I was over at her house a few days ago and saw a pic that you two took together. The second I laid eyes on you, it's like you captured my soul and held me captive. I must say, I was caught off guard because I've never done anything like this before. I'm not a weirdo or any kind of serial killer (joke). I am simply a man that recognizes a gorgeous woman and wants to be part of the reason she smiles. I would love to hear from you. You can hit me up at 404-698-3271 or shoot me a kite. I understand if you choose not to respond, but my gut tells me you will because you're just as curious as I am.

Love, Alonzo

Chapter Seven

Shayna Jackson

I stared down at the picture that was enclosed with this strange-ass letter. I sat there thinking I remembered my old bunkie Natasha. She was one of the few bitches that I actually dealt with. This was strange, though, because I couldn't remember her mentioning a cousin named Alonzo. I took another glance at the picture, wondering what this fool wanted with me, talking all this nonsense. I placed the pic and the letter back into the envelope and put it up under my mattress.

Days went by, and I couldn't get this man out of my mind. Those eyes seemed so familiar, like we'd met before. I wondered what he really wanted with me, so I decided to call him. I took out the envelope and walked over to the phone booth. I listened as he answered and the recorded message played out.

"Hello, Miss Shayna."

"Hello, Alonzo," I barely whispered.

"I've been waiting for your call."

"You sound confident; so tell me what you want from me. And I remember yo' cousin, but I don't recall her mentioning you."

"Yes, well, I was away overseas. My business takes me out of the country for months at a time."

Hmmm . . . Antennas went up in my head. A businessman; this might work out after all.

"If you don't mind me asking, what kind of work?"

"Ha-ha, I'm not at liberty to say at the moment, but Ms. Defense Attorney, I'll be sure to keep you on the payroll."

"Oh, I see. Say no more."

He went on, talking about how sexy I was and how he couldn't wait to meet me. I didn't say much on the phone. In my mind, I was too busy wondering why. I wasn't no fool; I needed to know what this man's interest in me was.

"Hey, Alonzo, your cousin gave me her number, but I misplaced it. Do you mind giving it to me? I would love to talk to her."

"No doubt. Give me a sec; let me pull it up. I'm sure she'd love to hear from you."

It seemed like he was telling the truth, because I called a bluff, and he didn't flinch. He read the numbers off to me, and before I could get a word in, the recording came on informing me that I only had fifteen seconds left. The phone cut off with us getting a chance to say good-bye.

I walked back to my bunk, smiling to myself.

"Say, bunkie, it looks like you got some good news," my nosy-ass bunkie said as she popped her head from under her cover.

I looked at her and smiled. This bitch never got the memo that I don't share my business with bottom feeders.

The man had me feeling good. He didn't know it, but he had ignited the fire in me. It was a great feeling to know that after all these years, a man still found me attractive. Shit, I knew I was a bad bitch, but being locked up had kind of put a damper on my parade.

I got on my bunk and lay down with my eyes closed. I replayed the sound of his sultry voice that sounded like Barry White. He spoke with confidence and a little cockiness. He reminded me of a younger version of Alijah.

Being the lawyer I was, I tried to figure out what he wanted from me. All kinds of different scenarios ran through my mind. I thought it might have been someone the feds sent to discredit my claim against Gonzalez. Shit, I was too damn smart if they thought that I would blow my only fucking chance of walking out of here months early by running my mouth to a nigga I didn't even know. Whoever he was, to me, he was just another regular-ass nigga that recognized that I was high bred.

I was tired of wracking my brain, so I got up and pulled out the piece of paper that I wrote his cousin's number on and dialed the number.

"Hey, Shayna; girl, how you been?"

"Hello, Natasha, I'm hanging in there, girl."

"Girl, I hear you. I'm so happy that I'm outta that hellhole. Ten years was damn sure enough fo' me."

"Um-hmm. You already know I'm not a criminal, so I have no understanding of why I got here in the first place. My lawyer still trying to get me home."

"Yeah, true. You one of the few people that prison is not for. Keep your head up; your day is coming. You didn't kill anybody, so they can't keep you forever. The worst part is behind you now."

"Aye, Natasha, what is yo' cousin's name again? It's right on the tip of my tongue," I lied.

"Girl, you must be talkin' about Alonzo. Don't tell me that fool contacted you. He saw a pic that we took on the courtyard, and, girl, he kept on saying he's goin' get you. He's a fool," she busted out laughing.

"I can't remember you mentioning his name, which is strange because we spent hours talking about your family and different things. I mean, I would've remembered if you did."

"Yes, please don't tell him that. He's my cousin on my dad's side. We were close growing up, but he spent most of his time gone."

"Oh, I see."

"Why you sound like that? Alonzo is a real good dude. He's on top shit; that's why I even bothered to give him your address. I know you could use a friend, especially after all you been through. Shit, he might be the one to hold you down while you're in there. I know you strong, and all, but even the strongest of us need somebody to lean on."

"Girl, you're right. I just don't trust these niggas. I was kind of suspicious at first because I didn't remember you talking about him. Thanks for clearing that up for me."

"Shayna, girl, don't be a stranger. Hit me up on Corrlinks—" she said before the phone cut off.

I never really liked that bitch Natasha, but she was one of the few that tried to be friendly to me. So my ass would half-tolerate her ass. Maybe it wouldn't hurt to see what was up with this cousin. He looked kind of young, but, oh well. I would love to have some young cock. I could mold him the way I want him. Shit, I will have him so gone over this old pussy that he won't have time to be worried about those young bitches. Age is nothing but a number, and I look damn good for my age.

Chapter Eight

Azir Jackson

Man, I really fucked with shorty; she came through for a nigga. I was sitting back chillin' when I got the phone call that I was hoping for. I was kind of nervous that the bitch wasn't going to call. From what I learned, this bitch wasn't no slouch, so I'm pretty sure she was trying to figure out where the fuck I popped up from out of the blue.

"Yo," I answered the unknown number.

"You have a collect call from a federal facility. Press zero to ignore, and five to accept the call."

My fingers couldn't move fast enough to press five. My first instinct was for me to go ham on this bitch, but I quickly caught myself. A soldier like me definitely knew how to play my position.

I was prepared for the question she was asking. From what I learned about her, I knew she wasn't no weak bitch, so I knew I had to get on her level. I could tell the bitch was full of herself from the minute she got on the phone.

I tried to convince her that I was legit and my only intention was to get to know her. I've always had a way wit' bitches, so dealing with her was no different. The only difference was this bitch was a poisonous snake. The kind that you got to cut they motherfucking head off. After I got off the phone with her, I felt confident that I'd be hearing from her on the regular.

A few days later, Natasha informed me that she called to check out my story. That right there let me know that she had some interest in me, which didn't surprise me. I made sure I gave hints about my status. That would grab the attention of a money-hungry bitch!

Everything was falling into place, but I had a few loose ends to tie up; then, hopefully, shit will start looking up for me.

It was the weekend, and I was feeling mellow. After a long week of putting in work, money was looking right. Shit, I scrolled through my phone to see which one of my bitches I was tryin'a chill with. I decided to call Shantè. She was a pretty little Panamanian bitch. I be fucking shorty, and she be talking that Spanish shit in my ear. I swear that shit sexy as hell, and it only made me fuck her harder. I dialed her number, and she picked up on the first ring.

"Aye, why the hell you've been ignoring my calls?"

"Babe, wha yuh a talk 'bout? I'd never ignore a beautiful woman like you."

"Uh-huh. I don't know what kind of shit you on, but you need to get it together before Miss Shantè be gone on that ass."

"Babe, you know I can't afford that; forgive me. Daddy will make it up to you."

"Hmm, let's see. I need a new Michael Kors bag and matching sandals."

"Shit, that's it? Yuh know mi have yuh, but yuh need fi do mi one favor first!"

"And what's that?"

"Come ride this wood fi yuh boy."

"That's easy. You know I will fuck and suck the black off that dick as long as you know I ain't fucking for free."

"Shit, we good then. I'm on the way to pick you up."

"All right, sweetie. I'll be ready."

I jumped out of bed and grabbed a pair of Levi's and a white wife beater out of the closet. Then I grabbed a quick shower and bounced. In no time, I was at her door in Clarkston. Before I'd left, I noticed Mom-dukes wasn't home, so I decided to take her to the house, 'cause she was always complaining that I always take her to the telly. Grandma was home, but she was cool as fuck. She 'ont really be on that bullshit.

After picking up shorty, we stopped at the Jamaican joint and grabbed us some food. I took her to the house. We smoked out in the truck, then went in and ate. She already knew what time it was. See, Shantè was one of those chicks that don't waste time on emotional shit. She's definitely a boss bitch. If I didn't know for a fact that she was a ho, I would've put her on my team.

"Come here, girl." I pulled her close to me.

"Hold on," she said as she took off her clothes. Shorty has a phat ass and some big-ass titties. Her pussy was also phat. She could've been a stripper for real.

"Let me ask you a question; why you never get into the stripping business?"

"Boy, no! That shit ain't no money. Then wit' niggas all disrespectful and shit, I wouldn't survive one night in there. That's chump change to me."

"A'ight, a'ight. Cool!"

"Take off your pants," she demanded.

"My bad."

I took my gun out of my waist and placed it in my dresser drawer. I was in my space, so I wasn't worried 'bout gettin' set up. Man, shorty made love to my wood like no other. She sucked, slurped, and swallowed every drop of come when I busted.

"Come here. Come ride dis wood." I motioned for her to get on top of me.

She was a bad bitch, 'cause most bitches I knew got on their knees to ride the wood; not shorty. She was on her feet, riding my wood. *Damn, she's a beast,* I thought.

Shit happened so fast that I didn't have time to react. I heard my Mom-duke's voice outside of the door. In a split second, she was standing in my room. Man, I was pissed the fuck off; I threw shorty off me.

"Yo, what the fuck is this? Why do you have this bitch in my house, Azir?" she yelled in front of the chick.

"Who the fuck she calling a bitch? Damn, what do you want to do? Fuck yo' own son, lady?"

"Yo, bitch, you need fi chill. Yuh a fool. Yuh can't talk to mi mother like dat."

"Boy, fuck you. Did you hear how she talked to me? I didn't know yo' grown ass was a mama's boy. Next time, find you a young-ass bitch to play around with."

"Man, can you get out so we could get dressed?" I asked in an aggravated tone.

I grabbed my boxers and pants and started to put them on. Shorty grilled on me as she put her dress back on. I tried not to make eye contact with her. I couldn't figure out if she was mad at Mom-Dukes or mad at me for checking her ass. Either way, I knew I needed to get her out of the house, 'cause the way Mom-dukes was fuming, it was liable to get physical any minute.

I heard Mom-dukes knocking on Grandma's door and going off on her. On some real nigga shit, she always complaining 'bout how I talk to her, but look at how she talks to Grandma. Grandma be calm and shit; I know she had to be tired of this shit too. Fuck, I know damn well I was tired of gettin' treated like a little boy. I have no idea how Grandma still deal with this shit.

I was about to step on the stairs when she blocked my path. Going on 'bout how I disrespect her. I really wasn't tryin'a hear none of that nonsense she was talking 'bout. I love that woman, but she didn't know when to shut the fuck up and stay in her place. I was tired of hearing her mouth, so I moved her out of the way and continued downstairs. She followed close behind, still cussing and carrying on. I opened the door and walked outside. Shorty was standing by the car, still pouting.

"Come on. Get in."

I pulled off, looked in my mirror, and I saw Mom-dukes standing out there, probably still running her mouth. God, that woman never shuts up, I thought.

"You know what, Azir? You dead-ass wrong for this shit."

"Hold on, lower your fucking voice. Now, how I'm wrong? I ain't know the woman was gonna come up in there," I said in an angry tone.

"You shouldn't have brought me to your house. You know yo' damn mother is a bitch!"

"Bitch, don't you ever call mi madda out of her pussyclaat name!" I backslapped her ass.

She busted out crying, but I didn't give a fuck. That bitch crossed the fuckin' line.

"Boy, fuck you! I'm done dealing wit' you. You lucky my brother Mickey is locked up; else you'd be fucking dead."

I pulled my gun and put it to her head. "Yo, B. I ain't tryin'a hurt you, right? So shut yuh pussyclaat mouf, man a bloodclaat bad, man. Yuh si mi." I watched as she shivered in her seat. I didn't want to body this bitch, but if she kept on running her motherfucking mouth, she would leave me no choice.

Then I sped through the streets, tryin'a get this bitch home. I burned tires and pulled up to the curb.

"Bitch, get the fuck outta my shit," I yelled.

"Boy, kiss my ass," she said as she jumped out of my truck.

I didn't respond. I pulled off. It was damn near four in the morning, and I wasn't tryin'a go home. I was angry and didn't want to hear shit Mom-dukes had to say. I called Tanisha.

"I'm on the way over to your crib."

"Oh, okay."

I fuck with shorty 'cause she never questions shit.

"I'm pulling up."

"All right."

She opened the door, and I walked in.

"You look mad. Everything all right?"

"I'm good. No sweat."

"All right, you need anything to drink?"

"Yea, something strong."

"All I got is Heineken and gin."

"Gi mi a shot of gin."

She handed me the glass, and I took the gin straight to the head in one big gulp. Then I rolled up a big head and sat there smoking.

"Damn, I can tell something's wrong wit' yo' ass."

"Nah, I'm good, but I'd feel better if you give me some of that fire head you got."

"Boy, not tonight. You need to chill and get whateva you're going through under control," she said and walked off. Minutes later, she returned. "Here go a blanket." She threw the blanket on me.

Damn! What's her problem? I thought. *These bitches be trippin' on a nigga.* I was gettin' tired of their old off-the-wall attitudes. I closed my eyes and let my mind wander off to a more serious issue at hand.

Sierra Rogers

The last time I felt like this was the day that I met Alijah. How could I forget that night he walked up in the salon? I lay on my back smiling; it was crazy how special I felt then, and here I was getting that same damn feeling. It was the kind of feeling that made my insides shiver and made my heart skip beats.

Exactly two weeks ago, I was out with one of the stylists. It's been years since I'd had any enjoyment. Tanya invited me to a family cook-out. My first instinct was to decline, but then I decided to go. I mean, what could it hurt? I needed to get out of the house for a little while anyway.

I did my hair the night before, choosing a long weave, and I went for a China doll look.

I decided to wear this little minidress from Nordstrom and a pair of Jimmy Choo pointy-toe pumps. I looked at myself in the mirror, and I hate to sound conceited, but, damn, a bitch was looking hot! I had to double back and look again. I ain't gonna lie; this was the best I was feeling in years. Let me find out I still got it, I thought as I sashayed downstairs.

"Hey Jeanette, I'm 'bout to step out for a minute."

"Oh, okay. You look nice; look like your old self. Remind me of me in my younger days."

"Jeanette, you're too funny. You *wish* you looked like this."

I looked at her. She wasn't no ugly lady, but after abusing drugs for so many years, she looked kind of pale. Wrinkles graced her face, and her lips looked burned.

"Child, please. Where the hell you think you get your looks from? I was one female to be reckoned with back in my day."

"If you say so. Don't wait up for me. I might not make it home."

"Thank you, Lord. I've been praying for this day to come. You're still young, and ever since Alijah died, you just gave up on yourself. It's time for you to get your life back. Start living and stop existing. Maybe you could find a nice young man and make me a few more grandchildren. Azir is grown now."

"Keep hoping, lady. My old ass won't be having any more children and damn sure ain't looking for no damn man."

I walked into the kitchen, grabbed my keys, and walked downstairs to the garage. I shook my head in disbelief. The things that came out of that lady's mouth was unbelievable. Damn. Babies! Her old ass better go get fucked and make some babies if she wants some.

I jumped in my car and pulled out of the driveway. I was definitely in a great mood, and the weather was nice. Good combination, I thought. I dialed Tanya's number so I could get her address.

"Hello, chica."

"Hey, babe, I'm just leaving the house now. Text me your address so I can put it in the GPS. You know I'm not from here," I laughed.

"No problem, and for the record, you've been living here more than five years. So, technically, you're a Georgia peach, shorty."

"Richmond, VA, 'til the day I die, baby love. Anyway, I'll see you in a few."

Tanya seemed like a cool-ass chick. She's been working for me for 'bout six years. She didn't act stuck up like some of these Georgia bitches. Some of them had the nerve to be calling themselves a damn Georgia peach. They asses looked more like Georgia monkeys. I put her address in the GPS and headed to her house in Lithonia.

I entered her street, and no lie; there were some big, nice-ass houses. It damn sure looked better than some of them old, worn-down houses I passed on my way in. The street was packed with cars, and I heard music.

"Your destination is on the left," the GPS sounded. I cut it off and pulled over on the side where I saw a parking space. I parked, looked at myself in the mirror, and made sure my hair was still looking good, and my lips were still glossy.

I grabbed my purse and my phone, then exited the car; I made sure the car was locked. I didn't know these people and damned sure wasn't going to trust them with my shit.

"Hey, girl, welcome to mi casa." Tanya ran toward me and hugged me.

"Thanks for inviting me. It beats sitting in the house watching another *Law & Order* marathon."

"Girl, c'mon. Everybody back here. Some of them drunk, so pay them ole fools no mind." I followed closely behind her.

"Hello, everybody. This is my boss Sierra. Say hello to her."

"Hello, Sierra, welcome to our home," they said in unison.

"Hello. Nice to meet y'all," I replied and smiled.

"Hello, beautiful," a sultry voice startled me from behind.

I turned around . . . and stood there at a loss for words.

"Sierra, this is my younger brother Dwayne," Tanya chimed in.

"I'm sorry. I didn't mean to stare. Hi, my name is Sierra," I said nervously.

"Bitch, get it together. You trippin'," a voice in my head warned.

He took my hand, kissed it, looked into my eyes, and said, "Hello, beautiful, I'm Dwayne."

I pulled my hand out of his. He was making me nervous. The brotha was around six feet two, brown-skinned with a clean shave. His body was well toned. The sleeveless shirt that he had on showed off his muscles.

"Dwayne, keep Sierra company while I check on the food. Don't wanna burn them damn burgers," Tanya said and walked off.

"Can I get you anything to drink?"

"Yeah, water is fine. Thank you."

"You sure you want water? Or you want something a li'l stronger?" he smiled at me, showing his pearly white thirty-twos.

"Hmm. You're right. Yeah, give me something a li'l stronger," I smiled back.

I was happy when he walked off. That gave me a chance to gather my composure. Damn! That nigga was fine!

"Here you go, love, and I brought you a chair. I figure your feet hurting in those heels."

"I see you're also a comedian, but thank you," I laughed.

For the rest of the evening, we talked and joked. He even rolled up a few blunts, and we smoked and drank Cîroc Vodka. This wasn't my intention, but it felt good to be in the presence of an attractive, intelligent brother. I could tell he was street, but not your average street nigga, which was definitely a plus. His conversation grabbed me and held me hostage for the entire evening.

"Damn, y'all deep in conversation over here. Girl, don't believe none of that shit he saying. He a slick one," Tanya interrupted.

"See, my sista is always a hater. Don't pay her no mind." We all busted out laughing.

"A'ight, I'm gone. Sierra, girl, let me know if you need anything."

"Okay, love. I'm fine. Dwayne is taking good care of me." I winked at her.

I was feeling extra good after I smoked that high-grade weed and drank two glasses of liquor.

The night was winding down, and I was getting tired. I glanced at my phone. It was exactly 8:30 p.m. I decided to stay a little longer before I called it a night.

"So, Sierra, what is a beautiful woman like you doing out without a man?"

"Dwayne, do you want to ask me if I have a man?" I looked him in the eyes and smirked.

"You got me. So do you?"

"No, I'm single," I blurted out.

"Oh, okay . . ." he smiled.

Man, at that moment I swear my body was reacting to his sexy voice. Until that moment, I didn't realize how long it had been since I'd had sex or been in the presence of a man. After Alijah died, I made a vow not to be with another man. I tried numerous times to come up out of that mind frame, but my heart wouldn't allow me to. This time was different, though. The way this nigga was making me feel, I considered getting rid of that vow! I was ready but not just with any man. The *right* one.

"So, Dwayne, you have a woman?"

"Nah, I got a chick that I chill wit' from time to time, but nothin' serious. I'm really looking for someone that I can start something serious with."

"Okay, I see."

This was definitely music to my ears. I was so caught up in our conversation that time flew past me. I glanced at my phone. Now, it was minutes to midnight. Wow, it's crazy when you are caught in an interesting conversation. You are not worried about time. I was starting to feel tired, though.

"Well, Dwayne, I'm 'bout to roll up outta here. It's getting late."

"Oh, okay, shit. I'm 'bout to hit the club in Atlanta. You tryin'a go?"

"No, maybe next time. I'm tired."

"Okay, shorty. Put my number in your phone. Hit me when you have time."

I took his number, hugged Tanya, and left. That was crazy. Everybody else had already left, and I was the last one to leave. He walked me to the car. We talked for a few more minutes; then I pulled off. Outside of Alijah, I've never met a man that held my attention that long. His conversations were not boring. He was kind of like a jokester, but I liked that. He kept me clinging to his every word that he was spitting out. I really needed that.

"Yo, make sure you use that number."

"No, you make sure you pick up," I laughed before I pulled off.

I was in a mellow mood as I drove down the street. I enjoyed myself at the cookout. The food was great, and Dwayne was jovial. He was one smooth brotha, I thought. In a split second, a rush of guilt swept over me. I knew the feeling all too well. Every time I tried to fix my mind to feel like I was ready to start dating, the guilt of betraying Alijah overwhelmed me. I cut the music on high as I tried to drown out those thoughts.

I pulled into the driveway and noticed Azir's truck parked on the side. *At least I can get some sleep tonight because he's not out there in those streets,* I thought.

I entered the house and went directly into my secret stash to get me some weed. I quickly rolled me a blunt and poured me a glass of Moscato. The house was quiet, so I assumed everyone was in for the night. I cut the lights off and headed upstairs. I was 'bout to enter my room when I heard a weird sound coming from Azir's room. I second-guessed myself and decided to ignore it, but the mother in me wouldn't let me walk away. I turned around and headed to his room. I didn't even knock. I pushed the door, it opened . . . and

I stood there in shock with my mouth wide open. My son was fucking a bitch in my house!

"What the fuck you doing in my house?"

"Damn, Ma, how the heck you get in here?" He pushed the naked slut off him.

"Azir, this is *my* fucking house, and you have no right bringing your bitch in here. You're too fucking disrespectful. Now get this bitch out of my house!" I screamed.

"I'm not goin' be too many bitches," this silly ho opened her mouth and hollered.

"Bitch! Shut the fuck up talkin' to my moms like that," Azir yelled at her retarded ass.

"Little girl, please put your clothes on and get your stanking ass out of my house before I catch a case up in here," I said and took a step closer to her ass.

She realized I was in no mood to be fucked with, so she grabbed her clothing.

"Damn, Ma. Close the door so we can get dressed."

I slammed the door without answering him.

"Open this door!" I banged on Jeanette's door.

"What the heck's going on?" She opened the door looking pissed.

"How the hell you're here and allowed Azir to be in my damn house wit' a bitch?"

"Sierra, what you talkin' 'bout?" She seemed puzzled.

"I just came home and heard sounds comin' from his room. I went to investigate, and they are in there fuckin' in my damn house," I yelled.

"Sierra, you need to calm down. I wasn't feeling good, so I turned in early. I had no idea Azir was here."

"So you're in a fucking house and have no idea who is in here wit' you? This is ridiculous," I said and walked off.

"Let's go! Get yo' ass out of my house." I yelled toward the room.

I stood in the hallway and waited until this little yellow bitch speed walked past me with Azir.

I blocked Azir's path so he couldn't go.

"Let me tell you something. I don't care how old you think you are; don't you ever come in my house disrespecting me like that."

"Ma, chill out. You wasn't even home."

"What the fuck that mean? You still brought that bitch into my house."

"Ma, no stress. I'ma get my own place ASAP," he said and snatched himself away from me.

I followed closely behind him, giving him a piece of my damn mind. I swear this boy done lost his fucking mind. He was grown, so if he wanted to have sex, he needed to get his own shit. Over my dead body was this shit going down under my roof.

I watched as he pulled off with that bitch on the passenger's side. Then I slammed the door and made sure it was locked. I turned off the light and proceeded upstairs.

I sighed as I sat on my bed. What was supposed to be a great night ended like this. I glanced at the clock and noticed it was after 1:00 a.m. I was so tired and drained. I lit up my blunt, took a few pulls, then put it out. After that, I crawled into bed, and the rest was history.

"Sierra, you might feel like I'm out of place, but maybe you need to try going at Azir differently," Jeanette suggested.

"What you mean? I've been nothing but good to this boy, and all he ever did is disrespect me. So what you saying?"

"Sierra, I'm not no expert on parenting, you know that. All I'm saying is if you keep on pushing him, you might push him out in these streets. You don't want to lose him forever."

I sat there looking at her . . . This bitch always thinks she knows all the right answers to parenting. It often leaves me baffled. When did she learn how to be a great fucking mother? Was it *after* she left me?

"I'm Azir's mother; I think I know what's best for my child, don't you think, Jeanette?"

"Yes, ma'am. I was only trying to make a suggestion. Didn't mean to offend you."

"I'm not offended. You just need to stay in yo' place. I got this. He's a rotten spoiled ass, and he's not gonna run in and out of my house. He's grown, so he should get out and get his own place; that way, he won't hear my mouth. And since you're such an advocate for Azir, maybe you can move in with him."

"Sierra, stop being so quick to get defensive. You're not too old to get advice. I know I messed up, and when I realized it, it was too late. It's not too late for you. Try to talk to him instead of yelling. Stop using Alijah's tragedy to influence your decisions. It's been years. Let it go; let him rest in peace and build a relationship with your only child," she said before she walked off.

"*I'm* pushing Azir in the street?" I mumbled to myself. Bullshit. He was in the streets in Jamaica. I wasn't trying to be his friend. I'm his damn mama, and I'm not—I repeat—I'm *not* going to let up until he gets it together.

I was missing my bitch. Days like these I wished she was closer. I definitely needed to make a trip home. Get away from everything for a few days. I picked up the phone and dialed her number.

"Hellurr," she mimicked Madea's voice.

"Hey, chica, what's going on?"

"Shit, just getting up. Lamar from Chamberlain Avenue had his annual Black and White affair last night. My ass be forgetting I ain't a little girl no more. I worked all day at the shop, then partied all night."

"Damn, I'm jealous. My ass is tired of being in the damn house all the damn time. Work and home; I feel old as hell."

"Bitch, ain't nobody told yo' ass to move to the country. Now you a country bitch. Why don't you hang out with the bitches at the salon?"

"Hell nah, you know damn well I don't do bitches and definitely not *these* country bitches."

"Well, you one of them so might as well join them." She busted out laughing.

"Whateva, you crazy bitch. Anyway, I'm just sitting here missing you and shit. Wish you were closer."

"Oh, I miss you too. I was just telling the bitches at the shop how I wish you was here."

"We need to talk more. I wish all this hadn't happened, and I was still in Richmond. Atlanta is cool, but ain't no place like Richmond."

"Sierra, something bothering you. What's going on? You all right?"

"Girl, it's Azir. Mo', I don't know what to say or do anymore." The tears escaped faster than I could wipe them away.

"What you mean? He all right?"

"He's in these streets, and I'm sick and tired of talking; it's like it's going in through one ear and out through the other. The other day, I found a gun and a bag of powdered coke under his mattress. Then when I confronted him, he has the nerve to tell me I was snooping."

"Girl, what? You lying. I thought he came back to go to school?"

"That's what he was supposed to do. But I blame Alijah's mother. After he turned eighteen, she gave him the account info, so he got all the money, and instead of him trying to get an education, he keep talking 'bout doing music."

"Girl, that bitch wrong for that. She know damn well you 'ont give no young boy all that damn money. I would've cussed her ass out."

"Girl, I don't even trip off that lady. He was down there giving her the same hard time, so she was happy to get rid of him, along with the money."

"Azir will learn about these streets. You think he'd learn after what happened to y'all."

"Girl, he walk 'round here all angry and shit. Half the time, I don't know where the fuck he at.

My damn heart be hurting every time the phone rings late at night, scared that I'll get a call that he locked up or dead." I cried louder.

"Sierra . . . I don't even know what to say. I have brothers, and you know they live in the damn streets, and it's the same way. My mother be begging them, but you can't do much, 'cause he grown. You can only hope for the best. Just the other day, Azir was a little baby. Now, he all grown. Girl, I 'ont know—"

"Mo', God knows I took one loss; I can't go on if anything happens to him. He don't know it, but he's hurting my heart. I lost his father, and I would rather die first before I lose my one child. But he is hardheaded, Mo'. He behaving like these streets are safe. I thought he would look at his father's situation and take heed. It's like he used that as a motivation for him to get deeper in the streets."

"Girl, wipe your tears. God goin' protect my god-baby. I couldn't bear if anything happens to him. He goin' be all right. He still young. He'll come around soon. Just put him in God's hands."

"Damn, bitch, you went all spiritual and shit," I busted out laughing. I could always count on Mo's ass to lighten up a mood.

"Shit, I wasn't tryin'a be funny. I'm for real. That's what all the Christian folks say when shit fucked up. I was just saying the same thing, and hoping it works for us. Shit, I can't lose my damn god-baby. "

"Well, I be praying hard for him. God brought me through two attempts on my life, so I know he can work this out for me."

"You ain't lying. You the only bitch I know that been shot twice and still was able to walk away from it. Bitch, you should've got baptized and somewhere wearing a nun dress and praising the Lord."

"Girl, I think about that shit all the time. The pain is still there, but I learned to cope. It could be worse."

"You ain't never heard anything about that stupid bitch?"

"Nope. Her ass supposed to be coming out soon."

"Really? I still don't understand why that ho didn't get life for what she did to you. I tell you, when motherfuckers got money to get big-ass lawyers, they can beat anything."

"Girl, you know they needed her ass to testify against Chuck and Dre."

"Oh shit, whatever happened to them?"

"They got life. They pled out to avoid the death penalty."

"That's fucked up. I tell you what; them niggas are two loyal muthafuckas."

"You ain't lying. Alijah knew it too. He loved them with everything in him. I used to write them, but as time went on, I kind of lost touch with them, and I realized that I needed to work on me."

"Yeah, girl, it was terrible, and I could never imagine what you went through, but you're still here and fighting. You one strong bitch, though. Anyway, how Jeanette doing?"

"She a'ight. I had to put her in her place the other day about Azir. She goin' tell me I need to be easy on him. Like, bitch, *really?* How can *she* give *me* any advice on parenting?"

"Yeah, Jeanette knows she dead wrong, but you know they say addicts get clean and totally forget that they were a piece of shit before. Then they behave holier than thou."

"Girl, you know I dug into her ass. Shit, don't get me wrong. She been clean for a minute, but that don't mean that I've forgotten the first twenty-something years that she smoked that shit. God knows I be trying to forgive her, 'cause she be there and shit. I just don't like when she put her two cent in about parenting."

"I feel you on that. Well, just keep pushing, and trust me, one day when we all old and shit, we goin' sit back and laugh 'bout most of this shit."

"Mo', man, you right. Enough 'bout me and my fucked-up-ass life. What's going on with you?"

"Girl, nothing. Working as usual, shop doing pretty well. Troy supposed to be home next month. So, you know I got to get my shit in order. Get all these other niggas out of the way. You know he 'ont play no games. My ass will be on lock when he gets home."

"Uh-huh, I feel you," I said.

We ended up talking for a little while longer, then hung up. Mo' always knew how to make me feel better at times.

Chapter Nine

Sierra Rogers

After calling Dwayne, we started hanging out. We would go out to eat, we went to the movies a few times, and he went to his house. It was hard adjusting being around another man, but as time went by, I started opening up to him. He made it easy on me; he wasn't pushy. The first time we kissed, I was the one that initiated it. The more time I spent with him, the stronger my feelings for him started getting.

"So we've been hanging around wit' each other for a while. Where do you plan on taking this?" he shocked me one evening while we were chilling.

"Huh? I don't know. I've been thinking the same thing, but I didn't want to come off pushy or thirsty."

"Nah, I'm definitely feeling you, and I love spending time with you. I think it's time we make it into something greater."

"Hmm, I love the sound of that."

I reached over and started kissing him to seal the deal. It really feels good that a man was feeling the same way I was feeling. After Alijah, I was so scared, but I think Alijah would want me to move on with my life. I mean, it's damn near twenty years now.

Dwayne and I became an item. I loved spending quiet moments with him. He was so attentive to me and my needs. It was like a breath of fresh air. I said I wasn't going to date another street nigga, but Dwayne was different. I ain't gonna lie, that nigga had me feeling like I was in my teenage years all over again. From the flowers delivered at work, to the late-night fuck sessions, he made it easy for me to fall for him. The crazy part was, I knew I was falling head in, but I didn't want to stop it. I never thought I could ever feel like this again, but he woke up something inside of me.

"Somebody around here is glowing," Jeanette said as I walked in the living room.

"Lady, what you talkin' 'bout now?" I gave her a strange look.

"Mmm-hmmm. I think you're in love," she said and turned back to watching the TV.

"You can tell just by looking at me?"

"Shoot! Even Ray Charles's blind ass could see that shit," she laughed out loud.

"I ain't goin' front; I really like him." I stooped down beside her on the couch.

"Hmm, and who is this 'him'? Whoever he is, he must be special. You been on cloud nine for 'bout a month now."

"You'll meet him soon. Ma, I mean, Jeanette, he's so different. He makes my heart skip beats, but sometimes when I remember Alijah, I get so depressed."

"Sierra, you deserve happiness. Alijah been gone, and one thing I know, he'd want you to move on wit' yo' life. I watched you for years beat yourself up. Let it go. You was Alijah's heartbeat, but he's gone. Baby girl, allow yourself to start living again, not just existing."

By the time she finished speaking, I was bawling my eyes out. I think this was what I needed. I needed to set my soul free of Alijah and my past. I could no longer hold on to a man that was never coming back. What Jeanette said had really touched my soul.

"Chile, wipe your tears and allow yourself to enjoy this man. I want to meet him so I can thank him for bringing some normalcy back to your life."

"You better not embarrass me. You'll meet him on Sunday. By the way, can you make some chicken alfredo casserole for us?"

"What you goin' do about Azir?"

"What you mean?"

"You know he has never seen you 'round any man before. You know how boys are with their mother."

"I ain't worried 'bout that. Azir is grown just like I am. I don't tell him which one of these little bitches to talk to, so ain't no way in hell he goin' tell me who to talk to. Plus, I ain't seen his ass since that day when he stormed out. I tried calling him, but he ignored my calls. I'm not going to stress myself out behind him."

"OK," Jeanette said and rubbed my back again.

"So, Jeanette, I haven't seen you with a man since I was a child. You don't get lonely?"

"Chile, I had my share of men when I was on crack. At my age right now, I can't see me dealing with these men and their bullshit."

"Jeanette, you got a point right there."

"Yeah, I've been through hell and back. If it wasn't for the grace of God, I would've been dead. I've been raped numerous times, and back in the day, I would've sucked and screwed just for a li'l piece of crack. These days, I focus on my recovery and giving my life to God."

"Wow! I never knew all that; I mean the rape. I have to give it to you; you've come a long way." I looked at her.

"Yeah, it's not easy, but you and Azir is part of that motivation. I hurt you enough when you were young. I can't change the past, but I be damned if I won't make our future better," she said with tears in her eyes. I didn't say anything; instead, I got up and walked upstairs.

I ain't gon' front. She was one strong woman. I saw how much she had grown from the time I was young, and she was cracked out. To be honest, she had been my rock throughout the years. With Mo' all the way in VA, I don't know what I would've done without her. Maybe it's time that I started to show her how grateful I was to have her in my life.

I got into my bed thinking that I was definitely in a great place in my life right now. I was finally feeling happy again. I didn't know where Dwayne and I were heading, but I wasn't in any rush. I was willing to ride the wave out; I wanted to take my time.

Damn! I was running late again. This Atlanta traffic was crucial, especially during rush hour. I had an 8:00 a.m. sew-in to do. I have to do better than this, I thought. Leaving from Dwayne's house in Buckhead and heading to the east was not good in the morning. I've been spending nights at his house on the regular. We talked 'bout moving in together, but I had no idea how that was going to work. We both had our own homes, and neither was trying to give it up. Well, we'll see how it goes.

I pulled up in the parking lot, quickly parked, and pranced into the shop.

"Good morning, chica," I said to Tanya.

"Good morning. You late, ain't you?" she laughed.

"Whew. That traffic on Twenty East ain't no joke."

"Hmm. You live in the east, so I take it you was at my brother's house." She looked at me for confirmation.

"Hmm . . . My lips are sealed," I said and walked off.

"Hello, Miss Rose. Sorry I'm late; I was stuck in traffic."

"Good morning, love. I know how it is. You made it safe; that's all that matters."

"C'mon, sit over here. Let me shampoo you."

I took about forty-five minutes to do Miss Rose's hair. She thanked me and left. I started straightening up my work area when Tanya walked over and leaned on the back of the chair. She shot me a sneaky look, and I looked at her. I was trying to figure out what was going on with her.

"Hmm . . . You know my li'l brother must be feeling you. He never, and I mean *never,* let no woman spend the night at his house. Hmm . . . I 'ont know what you did to him, but he is changing."

"Girl, it take a woman like me to change a player like him," I smiled at her.

"Yeah, I hope you can convince him to leave these streets alone. Mama been begging him. She already lost one son to the streets, but Dwayne ain't hearing her, though."

"Yeah, we talked 'bout that the other night. I know you don't know, but my son's father got killed in the streets, so I have strong feelings about that."

"Girl, I know. I lost my big brother; he was like a father figure to me. I still mourn him up to today. I can't go down *that* road again."

"Who you telling? Dwayne is my first serious relationship since I lost Alijah. He know how I feel 'bout it, so we'll see if he's serious 'bout me."

"Girl, I know his baby mama Tyreeka is mad as hell that he has moved on. I swear I can't stand that bitch—always starting drama in our family. She uses my nephew as a pawn, 'cause she knows my brother love that little boy. It's only because of my brother why I ain't whup that bitch ass already."

"Damn! She *that* bad? He told me there is bad blood between him and her, but I stay in my lane and don't ask no questions, 'cause I ain't got time for no baby mama drama."

"Girl, that bitch just can't accept that he moved on and don't want her stanking ass no more."

"Damn! You hate her ass."

"Nah, the bitch is scandalous. I'm surprised she don't pop up when you're there. Just watch that bitch."

"Hmm . . . That bitch better stay away. I would hate to show her ass that I ain't nothing to be fucked with. Plus, I'm too old for all this drama. I already went through hell with one ho. I be damned if I'ma put up wit' another psychotic bitch."

I finished straightening up, then glanced at the time. My next appointment won't be here for another half an hour.

"Girl, here come my eleven o'clock appointment. We'll talk later," she said and walked off.

I walked to my chair and sat down as I wondered what her motive was for telling me all that about the baby mama. See, her ass just didn't know that I didn't trust no bitch; and I sure didn't fuck with the in-laws. I bet you any amount of money her ass was cool with the baby mama and look how she dogging her out. I knew I had to watch *her* ass . . .

The weekend came around pretty quickly. I was off and decided to do a little shopping. It's been months since I bought anything new. I left Jeanette at the house cooking dinner. Dwayne was coming over for dinner and to finally meet her. I just hoped she didn't say much or try to embarrass me in front of him.

It felt great, spending some money. When I tell you my ass went in Macy's and spent close to a thousand dollars on jeans and some nice tops, I had to drag my ass out of that store. Then I hit up American Eagle, where I found a few shorts. I end up spending another $300. I was ready to leave the mall before I spend another dollar.

I stopped and got my truck washed and shampooed before I headed home. I was looking forward to this dinner. I grabbed all my bags as I exited the truck and headed into the house. The strong aroma of spices hit my nose as I walked through the house.

"Hmmm, it smell good up in here," I said as I walked into the kitchen.

"Yeah, I'm almost done. I made some chicken alfredo, oxtails, rice, macaroni and cheese, and cabbage."

"Damn! You went all the way out, huh?"

"Yes, ma'am. My future son-in-law is coming to dinner, so I have to make sure he's well fed."

"You is a trip," I laughed and walked out of the kitchen.

I took a shower and decided to put on a dress I had in my closet; nothing fancy, just comfortable. I put my weave into a bun, put a pair of my diamond studs in my ears, and put on a little face powder. It was simple but beautiful.

I heard the doorbell ringing, so I went downstairs to get it. I looked through the peephole and saw it was Dwayne.

"Hello, love," he said and gave me that smile that made a bitch instantly wet. *He better stop playing,* I thought.

"Come on in." I grabbed his hand and led him toward the kitchen.

"Hmmm," I cleared my throat, "Jeanette, this is the mystery man Dwayne—and, Dwayne, this is my mother, Jeanette."

"Wow! Nice to meet you, Miss Jeanette," he said and shook her hand.

"It's 'bout time and please do me a favor and leave the 'Miss' off my name." We all laughed.

"Okay, babe. C'mon, let's go in the living room until she warms up the dinner."

"Sierra, where's your manners? Did you ask him if he need something to drink?"

"No, but since you brought it up, I'll ask. Babe, you want something to drink? I got gin, Grey Goose, and wine."

"Yeah, lemme get Grey Goose on the rocks."

I rolled my eyes at Jeanette and fixed my man a drink and fixed me one too. I needed something strong to steady my nerves.

We then went into the living room to relax for a few minutes. I wanted some privacy so I can kiss all over him.

"You better stop playing around before yo' mama walk in on us," he said between kisses.

"I'm just saying, you can't blame me. Yo' ass just so fine." We busted out laughing and went back to kissing some more. I was thinking about taking his ass upstairs to my room, but before I could make that move, Jeanette hollered that dinner was ready. We looked at each other, laughed, and got up. He sat in the dining room, while I walked into the kitchen to help Jeanette. I took his plate to him, then grabbed mine.

"I'll be here shortly to sit, y'all," Jeanette said as she placed salad on the table.

"Man, yo' mama threw down."

"Yeah, she knows her way 'round the kitchen."

"Damn, do you know *your* way 'round the kitchen too?"

"I know a little sump'n sump'n," I laughed.

"The oxtails is bangin', boo."

"Yes, it is. I'ma need her to teach me how to cook it."

"Yes, 'cause I'ma need this kind of cooking on the regular."

"Mmm-hmm, you better stick with what you know," I busted out laughing.

My laughter was cut short when I heard the front door open. I looked to my right and saw Jeanette in the kitchen, so I knew it was Azir. Before I could say anything, he walked into the dining room.

"Hey, baby," I said.

"Whaddup, Ma? Who is this?"

"No, you 'ont do that. You walk in here and say hello first; then *maybe* you can ask me who he is."

"Whaddup, homie? I'm Dwayne," Dwayne said and stood up and tried to shake Azir's hand.

"Yo, boss, don't I know you from somewhere? I never forget a face."

"I doubt it. And I would've remembered if I met you."

"Word. So you messing with my moms?"

"Azir, cut it out. You're being very disrespectful right about now. You better get the hell on with that shit."

"I'm just saying. That's your man? 'Cause you brought this nigga up in here, in a house my pop's money bought, and y'all laughing and kickin' it up in here."

"Boy, get the fuck outta here."

I got up and pushed his ass out. By this time, I was fuming with anger. This fucking child of mine must've lost his fucking mind. I watched as he walked into the kitchen.

"Azir, you wrong! Why would you disrespect your mother and her company like that?" Jeanette said. Clearly, she was upset.

"Grandma, I ain't disrespect her. I was talkin' to the nigga. I mean, I'm tryin'a find what he want wit' her."

"Boy, shut up! Your mother is grown, and you're out of line. Right is right, and wrong is wrong."

I walked back into the dining room. Dwayne was getting up from the table.

"What you doing? You're leavin'?"

"Listen, ma, I'ma let you handle your situation wit' yo' son."

"What you mean? Ain't nothing to handle."

He continued to walk toward the door, and I followed behind him. "Dwayne, *that's* how you goin' do it?"

"Sierra, chill out. All I'm doing is removing myself from a situation that can turn out wrong."

I saw the sincerity in his eyes. This was my cue to let him go. "A'ight, bae. I'll be there later tonight."

"Bet," he said, jumped into his Charger, and pulled off.

I practically ran up in the house yelling, "Azir, where your ass at?"

I didn't see him downstairs, so I ran upstairs to his room. I pushed the door open. He was sitting on his bed talking on the phone.

"Get the fuck off the phone." I yanked that shit from his ear.

"Man, what you doin'? Chill out."

"No! I'm tired of your shit. You walked the fuck up in here and disrespected me and my company. I'm sick and tired of you and your fucked-up ways. Yo' ass need to find you somewhere to live, 'cause I refuse to live wit' you any longer."

"You mad over this nigga? How long you been seeing him anyway?"

"Boy, you not fuckin' gettin' it. I'm fuckin' grown. Who I date is none of your fuckin' business. One thing I won't tolerate is you disrespecting me. You hear me? You have until the end of the week to find you somewhere to live."

"I see how it is. You choosing dick over your seed. It's funny 'cause my pop's money bought this," he pointed to the walls in his room to signify the whole house.

"Alijah is fuckin' dead. He ain't coming back, so get the fuck over it. If he were here, you damn sure wouldn't talk to me like you do. He would've knocked your fuckin' head off."

"I know dude from somewhere."

Right then, his phone rang, and he got up to pick it up off the floor.

"Oh yeah. I knew that's where I knew that nigga from. Yeah, that's him. A'ight, fam." He hung up his phone.

He then turned to me and laughed sarcastically. "You know what's crazy? You done sat here and ridiculed me every day for being in the streets, but here you are messing around with one of the biggest dope boys in the ATL. That's being a hypocrite. I *knew* I knew that nigga; just had to remember from where. You brought that nigga to the house; you don't know who he got beef with."

"Azir, stay the fuck out of my life. This is *my* house, and I will bring whoever I choose up in here. I mean it; find somewhere to live by Friday." I slammed the door behind me.

I stormed down the hallway and bumped into Jeanette standing by the stairs. I was too fucking pissed even to acknowledge her.

"Sierra—" Jeanette tried to say something.

"Not right now," I cut her off and stormed past her.

I went into my room and locked the door; then I let out a deep sigh. I was mad as fuck. This shit couldn't possibly be happening. This boy really tried me and to add insult to injury, called me a hypocrite. Just because I fuck a dope boy doesn't mean I want my child to be one. I was fucking done. Until he got his shit in order, I refused to deal with him.

I lay in bed for a good two hours, just thinking about Dwayne and what he did for a living. I wondered if I wanted to go down that same route again. I vowed that I would never mess with another dope boy, but this wasn't planned; it just happened. I had another chance to experience real love, and here this boy was trying to mess it up for me! I took a shower, put on some shorts and a wife beater, grabbed my pocketbook, and left the house.

I used the key he gave me to open the door. I didn't see his car in the driveway, so I figured he wasn't home. I went inside and went into the bedroom. It was empty, so I dialed his number.

"Yo, whaddup?"

"Hey, babe, I'm at your house."

"A'ight, cool. I got one more run to make; then I'll be there."

"Okay, cool."

I tried to figure out what kind of mood he was in. He didn't seem upset, which was great because I had something planned for him.

I lit the candles that I brought and placed them all over the room, put some slow jams on, took off my clothes, and put on my sexy Victoria's Secret lingerie.

It didn't take long for him to get to the house. I listened as he walked up the stairs. I got up, ran bathwater, and lit candles around his Jacuzzi.

"Babe, where you at?" he yelled out.

"Take off your clothes."

"Huh?"

"You heard me. Come on." I motioned toward the bathroom.

"Get in," I demanded.

He got in, and I started to wash him down. "Relax and close your eyes."

I washed his chest, then went down to his dick. I gently washed his dick while I massaged his balls. I could tell he was enjoying himself, 'cause he let out a slight growl. I finished washing him, let out the water, and filled it back up. Then I rinsed his body off.

"C'mon, babe."

I threw him a towel and walked into the room. After he dried off, he sat down on the bed.

"Lie down."

By this time, John Legend's song "All of Me" was blasting through the surround system. I grabbed my African Pride Oil and started rubbing him from his chest down. I massaged his dick and his balls. After I finished, I started kissing his chest.

"Damn, boo, what a nigga did to deserve this?"

"Shhh. Relax, I got this."

I walked over to his dresser where I had the whipped cream. I squeezed some out on the tip of his dick; then I knelt down and slowly licked it off. I used my tongue to spread it all down his ten-inch dick. I squirted some more on his balls, and I slowly took each ball in my mouth. He grabbed my weave as his toes balled up.

"Shorty, come here."

"Not yet."

I sucked his dick so damn good he couldn't hold back anymore, and he bust all in my mouth. I didn't shift; I opened my mouth wide as he squirted every ounce of his juice down my throat. I swallowed every drop and used my tongue to clean his dick off, which instantly made his manhood hard again. That's when I got on him and slowly slid down on his dick. I tightened up my muscles and squeezed down on every inch of dick God gave him. While doing this, I started to fondle my breasts and seductively lick them.

I guess he had enough, 'cause he slung me off him in an aggressive manner. He then pushed me down on my stomach and slid his dick into my sugar hole.

"Aargh, aargh," I moaned.

Damn, I thought I was the shit; that was until he applied pressure. I tried to climb up in the bed, at least try to eliminate some of the pressure, but I couldn't move. He held me around my stomach and pulled my ass toward him. Being the bad bitch I was, I had no choice but to throw that ass back and take the dick.

"Whose pussy is this?"

"Yours, daddy."

"A'ight, then, take this dick."

This nigga then flipped me on my back; I swear he was acting as if I were a rag doll. He threw my legs on his shoulders, then slid into my wet pussy. He banged out my walls for a good thirty minutes nonstop. When he was finished, I ran to the bathroom to run cold water on it. My pussy was burning from that dick whipping it took. The saying be careful of what you wish for was really true.

We got into the shower together, and after we washed each other off, we got into bed holding each other. "God, thank you for sending him," I whispered, right before I dozed off.

The next morning, I got up early. I had to head to the east, and, Lord, the traffic on a Monday morning was no joke. I tried to tiptoe around the room. I didn't want to wake him after all the work he put in last night. I grabbed my pocketbook and keys, about to leave.

"Sierra," he called out to me.

"Babe, did I wake you up? I was trying to be quiet."

"Nah, I'm good. I need to holla at you right quick."

"Oh, okay." I walked back to the bed.

My heart sank. After what happened yesterday, I wondered if he was going to tell me that he couldn't fuck wit' me.

I sat down beside him and turned my full attention to him.

"Listen, yo, I fucks wit' you on some real shit. I ain't never met another female of yo' caliber, and that's what a nigga need. Shit, after the way you fucked me last night, I'm convinced that I need you in my life."

"Wow! That's deep. I thought after yesterday, you didn't want to fuck wit' me."

"Listen up. I mean, I can't front. I was irritated as fuck 'cause li'l dude disrespected you. But I feel where he comin' from. I was once him; I even tried to shoot my stepdaddy, so that's minor."

"Yeah, you know Azir took his father's death real seriously. You're the first man that he done ever seen me with. I'm not excusing his behavior yesterday, though; he was dead-ass wrong."

"I mean, li'l homie still young, so he still has a lot to learn. If it was anyone else yesterday, I would've bodied him."

"I'm glad you didn't try to do anything to him, 'cause I would've killed you. That's my only seed." I looked at him with conviction.

"Ha-ha, chill out, ma. You out of your league. Trust me. But that shit sexy as fuck. Make me want to fuck you real hard and show you who the boss is 'round here. This is *my* city."

"Speaking of city, Azir claimed he know you, and you is a dope boy. I already told you how I feel about that."

"C'mon, ma. This all I know right here. This my life. This is how I feed my family."

"I understand that, but I've been down this road before, and God knows I can't go back down there. I care too much about you, and we both know there's only one or two outcomes when you're in the streets. I just can't," I said, shaking my head no.

He sat up in bed and turned my face around to him. "Listen, ma, don't be talkin' like that. I ain't goin' nowhere. Furthermore, I don't ever be out there like that. I stay on the low. Sierra, I fucks wit' you, shorty. Trust me; I want a life with you."

"Yeah, listen, I got to go. I'm opening up the shop today. In order for us to be, you need to leave the streets alone. I want a life of happiness, not burying another nigga or visiting him behind bars." I got up and walked out.

I hated to leave on a sour note, but I swear I couldn't let him think it was all good. I mean, I love these hood niggas, but I didn't like the way they fucked up their lives.

I got into my car and drove off. There I was, involved with another street nigga. I had no idea why I couldn't find me a good working-class nigga or something.

K. Michelle's "Can't Raise a Man" song blasted through my speakers. Fuck being a bottom bitch. Wifey was the position that I wanted. I no longer wanted to be the bitch that was visiting niggas in jail. Back then, I was proud to be Alijah's bottom bitch. But all that shit got me was a broken heart; I was not gonna sit back and let history repeat itself!

Azir Jackson

I was angry that Mom-dukes had that nigga in the house. On some real shit, I felt like my pop's money bought the house, so no nigga had the right to be up in there. To top it off, this nigga was a fuck nigga. I never forgot a face, and this nigga was familiar. I couldn't figure it out until my homeboy dragged my memory. I knew the nigga 'cause he was one of the pussyholes that had a problem wit' us opening shop out here. So imagine the shock when I found out that he was possibly fuckin' my moms.

I was tight wit' her 'cause every fuckin' day she got up preaching all that holy shit in my ear 'bout staying out of the streets, but look who she fuckin' wit'. One of the biggest dope boys. On some real nigga shit, that's why I 'ont be tryin'a hear all that shit she be spittin'.

On the real, I wanted to kill that nigga, but I was smart to know it wouldn't be a good move. I ain't trippin', though.

I was up early. First things first. I needed to get my own place. Mom-dukes and I was bumping heads too much, and I was tired of that shit. No disrespect to the woman, but she be trippin' over nothing on some real nigga shit.

I called up this real estate bitch that I used to fuck out in Norcross.

"Mr. Azir, what can I do for you this morning?" Her Trinidadian accent boomed through my phone.

"Hello, love. I need a huge favor."

"And what might that be?" she inquired while laughing.

"Take your mind out of the gutta, love. I need a two-bedroom condo ASAP."

"Cash or mortgage?"

"You already know what it is. Straight up dollars. I ain't got no job or credit; you know that."

"That's right. You're a businessman without proof," she laughed.

"Yeah, somethin' like that, but listen up. I need it ASAP. Like yesterday," I stressed.

"Okay, let me see what I can do. Do you have a preferred area?"

"Uuuum, anywhere in the east, Stone Mountain or Lithonia, preferably."

"Alrighty. I'll get back with you in a few days."

"Listen, Shari, hook a nigga up, and I got ten stacks for you outside of your commission."

"Alrighty, sweetie." She hung up.

Yes, *that's* what I was talkin' 'bout. I was beginning to like the idea of moving out into my own shit. Shit, I've been meaning to but was too busy handling some business. Damn, the number of bitches I could fuck without having to worry 'bout Mom-dukes running up in my shit . . . Now that this house shit was handled, I can turn my focus back to other more important shit.

I went through the trap and dropped some work off.

"Wha gwaan, brethren?" I dapped Jah T.

"Mid eh ya fadda. Weh yuh de pon?"

"Nothin' much. Droppin' off work and pickin' up some paper."

"Yeah, it's been jumpin' all morning! Yo, brethren, you sound upset when you call askin' 'bout dat nigga Dwayne. What the fuck going on?"

"Yo, yuh nah go believe dis. Mi walk inna Mom-duke's crib, and this pussyclaat sitting down with my moms laughing and talking."

"Nah! You lying."

"Hell nah! I'm dead-ass."

"Yo, yuh moms fuckin' wit' yo' enemy. That's crazy, yo."

"Man, fuck that. Shit ain't even funny, yo."

"Yuh tink 'im kno' dat's your madda?"

"Nah. There's no way he could've known, but fuck if he knew or not. He know now. Yo, I'll body that nigga and his whole family if he ever hurt a fuckin' hair on my mom's head. I'm dead-ass, yo!"

"I feel you on that. I know you tight 'bout that shit."

"Hell yeah, I am; then she put me out behind this bloodclaat nigga."

"Damn! She must feelin' him somethin' serious to do that."

"I ain't trippin'. I was already gettin' my own shit. I'm just tight that it's behind this pussyhole. Yo, on e'erything I love, I'll body that nigga!" I yelled.

"Yo, calm down and hit this." He handed me a spliff.

I took a few pulls. The ganja romanced my brain. I was hoping it would lower my anger level, but instead, it elevated it.

"Yo, hold this. I'm out. I'ma holla at you." I walked out of the trap and jumped in my ride.

I knew exactly where I was heading. I didn't give a fuck how it was goin' to end. I drove down

Panola and jumped on I-20. In no time, I was getting off on the Candler Road exit. I knew I was in this nigga's hood and out of my comfort zone. I had my gun on me, plus two extra clips, just in case some shit popped off. I pulled up at the rims shop that I knew this nigga would be at. I got out of the car and stomped inside.

"Sir, may I help you?" the bitch behind the counter called out.

By this time, this pussyhole nigga walked from the back. Our eyes locked like two pit bulls ready to attack.

"It's okay, Desiree. He's here to see me. Excuse us for a second."

Desiree shot me a dirty look before disappearing behind the door.

"Yo, what the fuck you doing coming up in my place of business like this?"

"Yo, son, fuck that! You straight violated me when yuh entered mi fuckin' house. So fuck yo' place of business."

"Yo, youngin', what the fuck you want? 'Cause I'm two seconds away from blowing yo' fuckin' brains out all over this concrete."

"Yo, B, you 'ont know who the fuck yuh dealing with. Don't let this young shit fool you. You 'ont watch the news. Young niggas takin' over. You heard?"

"Yo, your mom know you here?"

"I'm grown as fuck, yo; listen, homie, I want you to stay the fuck away from my moms, yo."

"Ha-ha! Who the fuck you think you talkin' to? I'ma fuck that bitch e'ery fuckin' day that I breathe. Li'l nigga, that pussy some fire for real. Don't worry, though; I'll treat that pussy good."

I pulled my gun and aimed it at his dome. "Pussyhole, go suck yuh mama. Try me, pussy-hole."

"Nigga, do it!"

I straight stared that nigga in his eyes, gritting hard as hell on him.

"Yeah, I thought so. You a little bitch just like your mom. Only thing is, she got a pussy. Yo, get the fuck outta my shit before that bitch got to visit the morgue tonight."

"Ha-ha. I got your nigga, on my pop's soul." I took a step closer to him.

"Yo, fuck yo' pops. I heard that nigga didn't know what to do with the pussy, but *I* got it. *I* be all through it. All in it," he laughed.

I was about to squeeze off when the reception-ist bitch walked from behind the doors. I looked up and saw all the cameras from every angle. I wanted to kill that motherfucker, but it wouldn't be a good move. I decided against it. I knew I could catch this nigga slipping when he least expected it.

I lowered my gun and walked out. Then I jumped in my car and sped off. This nigga had just signed his death warrant, and he didn't even know it.

A few days later, I was at a hotel chilling, counting my paper, thinking 'bout my life and plotting on how to get this nigga Dwayne. I couldn't eat, shit, or sleep without thinking 'bout this fuck nigga. My cell started ringing, bringing me out of the trance that I was in.

"Hello."

"Hello. I found you a three-bedroom condo out in Conyers. I tried to find a two-bedroom like you asked but had no luck. The price is pretty good, so if you're interested, I'll forward these pics over so you can see them; then we can meet up so I can show you the property."

"That's what the fuck I'm talkin' 'bout. I'm ready to see it when you're ready."

"Okay. Let's make it for Thursday at 10:00 a.m. I'll text you the address."

"All right, cool. Aye, when you goin' let me taste that pussy again?"

"Azir, please. When you stop being a dog. Until then, stay in your lane," she laughed and hung up.

Things were finally starting to fall into place for me. I smiled and continued counting my paper. Shit, I was happy that I was finally getting my own crib. Endless fucking and sucking. Everything was good, business was booming, and I was livin' the life.

I hadn't seen Mom-dukes since that shit popped off. My grandma called my phone to talk, which was cool, 'cause Grandma don't be on that bullshit like Mom-dukes. I was gonna wait 'til she was at work to go pick up my clothes. In the meantime, I took a shower, got dressed, and decided to hit the mall and got me a few outfits, mainly sneakers and drawers. I parked and got out of my ride when my phone started ringing. I looked down and realized it was my nana calling from Jamaica.

"Oooh," I said before I pressed *answer*.

"Hey, Nana."

"Hey, baby. How you doing?"

"Mi deh yah, a gwaan hold a meds."

"You register for school yet?"

"Nana, come on, mon. Mi tell yuh sey a mi music mi a pree."

"Bwoy, yuh need fi get yuh education. Music can follow after. Yuh take all dat money and squander it. Alijah neva put himself inna danger fi mek all dat money fi yuh waste it on foolishness," she scolded.

"Nana, chill out. I ain't wasting his money. I 'ont even spend it. I got my own paper."

"Where da hell yuh get money from? You don't have nuh job. So it's true; yuh out dere in di streets. Azir, yuh break mi heart. Mi raise yuh betta than dat."

"Nana, man, c'mon wit' all that. Mi nuh know what kind of lies mi madda a call and tell yuh. She just mad because mi nuh waan go nuh school, and mi want do mi own ting. Since she want to tell all dat, did she tell yuh she have man up in a di house?"

"Azir, yuh too outta order. Regardless of what you feel 'bout you madda, she bring yuh inna dis world. Me and her don't always see eye-to-eye, but one ting mi know sey; she love yuh wit' all her heart. Yuh need fi start showing her dat yuh care. Yuh is all she 'ave left. The Bible say 'Honor your madda and fadda and yuh days will be long.' Yuh too hardheaded, just like yuh fadda."

This was the first time in years that I had ever dropped a single tear. There was something 'bout my nana's words and the way she spit it out. It's like it ripped through my heart. Shit, it took a lot for me to feel any emotion about the shit that I've been through my whole life, but my nana, that woman was good with words.

"A'ight, Nana. I hear you," I said. I was very careful not to let her notice that I had shed a few tears. I loved my nana and didn't want to disappoint her. She was the only person that I would lie to so I can protect her feelings.

"Mi wan' yuh fi do more dan feel mi. Mi nuh 'ave long pon dis earth, but before mi go, mi wan' yuh and yuh madda fi mend tings."

See, my nana killed me with this righteous talking. She has been yelling that she was dying since I was a yute. And the funny part is, she actually believed this.

"Nana, yuh kno' mi nuh like when you talk like dat. Yuh nah go no wey."

My phone started to beep.

"All right, Nana. I got to go. I love you," I said, before hanging up on her ass.

Some of the best news I had gotten in weeks was when the realtor called me to do the paperwork on the crib. The shit was nice and suitable for a smooth nigga like me. I paid her a hundred and twenty-five grand, and I threw her ten stacks on the side. When it was all said and done, she handed me my keys.

"Aye, you know I need a woman to add her touch to it." I winked at her.

"Hmm, those hoes are lined up. You better start looking." She walked off on me.

Damn! That ass phat as fuck, I thought as she drove off.

Days later, I found me a professional decorator. I didn't have the time, and I didn't know anything 'bout fixing the condo up. I ordered furniture, and she put her feminine touch to it. I was proud when she was done. Before you knew it, everything was settled. I even brought this bitch home from Atlanta. We fucked all night from downstairs to upstairs. Talk 'bout breaking the house in. We did just that.

I drove to my Mom-duke's job and saw her truck, so I knew she was at work. I then headed to her crib so I could grab my clothes. As I pulled up, I took a long breath and rang the doorbell.

"Who is it?" my nana asked.

"It's Azir, Nana."

"Oh, baby. I didn't know you was stopping by." She reached out and hugged me tightly. One thing about Nana, she was very affectionate when it comes down to me.

"Mi just wan' grab mi stuff dem before yuh daughter get home."

"Well, come on, and do you mean your mother? Azir, I know it's rough on both of y'all, but Sierra love you. I really think y'all need to talk."

"Nana, mi good still enuh. Mi just wan' get the clothes."

I walked off, leaving her standing in the living room. I grabbed some big black bags from the kitchen and ran up the stairs. I was trying to hurry, 'cause the last thing I needed was Mom-dukes popping up. I didn't feel like seeing her or having to go through some argument shit right now.

"A'ight, Nana. Mi 'ave e'erythin'. I love you."

She grabbed my shoulder and stopped me. "You know we love you, and this will *always* be your home. Please call me so that I can know you okay. Azir, I love you," she said with tears rolling down her face.

"Love you too, Nana."

I hugged her, then left. I just needed to go . . .

I breezed through the trap to holla at my part-nas. Ever since I got the crib, I've been relaxing a little. I was enjoying the quietness of having my own shit, and, God, it was so good not to hear Mom's constant bickering.

"Yo, whaddup, Boss man?"

"Shit, how the drop went yesterday?"

"Everything went smooth. Bigga got one of them things."

"All right. That's what's good."

"Yo, brethren, I'm about to make a move. Gwaan hold down di spot fi mi. I'll hit yuh up lata."

I left the trap, jumped in my ride, and drove. I had one destination in mind. I've put off handing the situation, but the time was now to get it over with 'cause this bitch keep blowing up my phone, pretending like shit sweet between us.

I used my burner phone, which was the phone that I used to call my hoes. The bitch picked up on the first ring.

"Hey, babe," this snake-ass bitch answered.

"Hey, love, I'm coming through to see my favorite lady," I said.

"It's 'bout time. Can't wait to see you, daddy."

"I bet you can't, baby girl," I laughed.

I got to the crib in no time. She opened the door fast as hell. She went to hug me, and I backed up. I pulled my gun and pointed it at her.

"Babe, what are you doing?" she looked puzzled.

"Bitch, shut up and sit down. Don't let me hurt you for real. A'ight, now, this where we at. The last time I was over here, you set me up to get robbed. At first, I couldn't believe a bitch that I cared for would actually fuck me over like that. But as much as I want to believe different, shit is right in front of me. The way the nigga walked up on me let me know that. Somebody let him know I was comin' out and to top it off, I seen you lookin' out the motherfuckin' window when I pulled off."

"Azir, I swear, I didn't know you got robbed. I swear to you. I would never do that to you."

"Bitch, shut up! What the fuck that nigga gave you for settin' me up?"

"Azir, oh my God. You wrong. I love you too much. I would never do that," she cried.

"Listen up, you stupid ho, I'm dead-ass serious. You tell me the truth, I won't harm you, but if you keep on lyin', I'ma blow yo' bloodclaat head off and keep it moving," I said through clenched teeth.

I think she saw the anger in my eyes and knew right then that playtime was over. I lifted my gun and aimed it at her dome.

"Okay, okay, Azir, I'll tell you everything. Just don't shoot," she bawled.

"A'ight, bitch, you got five minutes to spit it out, and I'll let you continue breathing."

"Killa T and his boys approached me a few months back. They said they had an eye on you and knew that you was the big man. I tried to tell them I didn't know anything about what you do. He persisted and threatened me and my family. Azir, I swear to you, I was scared for my life," she hollered more.

I walked over to her and put my arms around her. "Dry your tears, baby girl," I said as I hugged her.

"I'm sorry, Azir. I swear I didn't mean to hurt you. I love you."

"Nah, babe, quit all that crying. If you're truly sorry, I need you to prove it to me." I looked her dead in her eyes.

"Yes! Anything, Azir. I'll show you how sorry I am."

"I need you to stop crying first." I wiped her tears before I continued.

"This what I need you to do. Call this nigga and tell him you got some more info 'bout how he can get some more money. Tell him you need to talk to him in person."

"Azir, Killa T is crazy. He'll kill me if he find out I'm lying."

"Shorty, you know I wouldn't let a nigga do shit to harm you. You my woman, and I'll protect you 'til the breath leaves my body."

"Okay, Azir, I'll call him right now."

After she left for the bathroom, I took out my silencer and put it on my burner. I walked over to the blinds and peeped outside. I had to make sure there were not a lot of people outside. I peeped a figure walking toward her complex. As he got closer, I noticed it was the same nigga that robbed me.

"Yo, c'mon. Here go the nigga." I grabbed her and shoved her toward the door.

"Answer that shit and act like you gotta hit for him. You know how you do."

I stepped into the kitchen before she opened the door.

"Hey, babe," he said and kissed her.

"Hey," she said dryly.

"So you got something for me? That's what I'm talking 'bout. I'ma give you this dick real good tonight."

"Yeah. I found out where Azir stash house at."

"You lying?"

"No . . ."

"Yeah, nigga, she lying." I stepped out of the kitchen with my gun aimed directly at this nigga. I kept my eyes on his hands.

"Yo, what the fuck is this? Bitch, what the fuck! You set me up?" He looked at her with his eyes opened wide.

"Pussyhole, let me get that up off you," I said and grabbed his gun from his waist.

"Bitch, I'ma kill you. You set me the fuck up," he yelled.

"Yeah, partner, she set you up. You know these hoes ain't loyal. I was feeling her just like you was, so why you think she wouldn't do to you what she did to me?"

"Man, fuck that shit you talking. What the fuck you want? You want your work and money back? I got them in the back of the apartment."

"Nah, partner, I want yah fucking life." I pulled the trigger twice, hitting him in the face. He fell to the floor, and I walked over and fired another round in his head.

"Noooo! Noooo! Noooo!" she screamed. "You killed him." She ran to his dead body and bent down, hugging him.

She was so preoccupied with that dead nigga that she didn't see the bullet coming toward her. I fired a single shot to the back of her head, killing her instantly. I checked her, then hawked and spit on that ho.

Quickly, I opened the door and disappeared into the back where my truck was parked.

Chapter Ten

Sierra Rogers

Jeanette told me that Azir stopped by to get his clothes. I was kind of shocked because I didn't know that he was trying to move out. I mean, he said it, but I didn't take his ass seriously. I can't say I wasn't feeling fucked by this. I called Azir earlier to see how he was doing, and he informed me he had his own place. To say I was shocked would be an understatement. I understand that I told him to get out, but that was only because I was angry. Deep down, I didn't want him to leave. At least when he's home, I know he's all right. I wish Azir and I could be closer. I miss my baby boy, and I knew there was a lot of pain between us. I just need him to understand that I wanted the best for him. I didn't want these streets to swallow him up; I wanted him to make something of himself. I knew he was grown, but he was still my baby boy.

***

It was a busy day at the salon. I couldn't complain, because I was making money. I noticed Tanya was kind of quiet. I walked in and said hello, and she barely mumbled under her breath. Throughout the day, she barely said anything to me, which was strange. On a regular day, I couldn't get her to shut up. I had no idea what was going on with that ho; all I knew was she better get her act right, 'cause I was in no mood to tolerate a miserable bitch.

By the time nine o'clock rolled around, I was beat. It didn't help that Jeanette made pot roast and sweet potato pie. I was stuffed. I couldn't continue living like this if I wanted to keep my shape. I decided to go to bed early, but first I had to catch the ten o'clock news. I cut it on, just in time to catch the weather woman saying it was going to be ninety degrees the next day. I hate the cold, but Atlanta was burning up. My electric bill was damn well near four hundred dollars. "*A twenty-one-year-old woman, Diamond Brown, and her fiancé were found dead in her apartment. I spoke to the homicide detective right before I came on the air, and I have to say the death of these two young people has rocked this quiet community. The police are asking the public to come forward with anything to bring their killer or killers to justice.*" Soon as I heard the name, I turned my attention to the television.

"Oh my God," I screamed out as I fumbled on the couch to find my phone.

I couldn't press the *send* button fast enough. Azir didn't pick up his phone, so I called right back. I wasn't sure if he heard the news.

"Hey, Ma." He sounded annoyed.

"Baby, I hope you're sitting down."

"Nah, why? What's going on?"

"When is the last time you seen Diamond?"

"I 'ont know. I don't mess wit' her like that."

"Well, she was murdered this morning, she and a guy."

"Damn! That's messed up," he replied nonchalantly.

"The girl that you've been seeing is dead, and all you can say is 'damn'? *Really?*"

"Ma, what you want me to say? She wasn't my chick. You even said she was with a dude when she was killed. I mean, that's messed up, but it ain't my problem."

"Azir, let me ask you a question. You don't know nothing about this, right?"

"Hell nah, Ma. Yuh trippin' now. That's why you call me—to see if I did it? Damn, you must think I'm a monster."

"Azir, no, I don't think you're a monster. I just wanted to make sure yo' name ain't mixed up in this mess. That poor child. I feel for her family, her poor mother. I can't imagine the pain she's feeling."

"Listen, Ma, I'm sorry to hear this, but I'm in the middle of something. I'll call you later."

"A'ight, Azir. Stay outta them damn streets. Love you, baby."

"Love you, Ma," he said before hanging up.

After I got off the phone, I lay back for a second. It bothered me how nonchalant Azir was about her death. Even if she'd moved on, I thought they were still friends. He seemed so cold and heartless about it, I thought.

I noticed how late it was, so I decided to go upstairs to bed. I looked at my phone, checking to see if I had any missed calls. I hadn't heard from Dwayne all day, and just like his sister's behavior, that was weird. Since we'd been dating, not one day went by without us talking. I'd tried to call him since this morning, but his phone just kept ringing. I hope he's okay because I know how dangerous it was in those streets. I made sure my ringer was on and got into bed.

The next morning, I was up bright and early. The first thing I did was grab my phone and look at it. I had no missed calls or texts. This was bothering me now. I thought 'bout callin' his sister but decided not to. I didn't want that bitch in my business anyway.

I took a shower and got dressed. I needed to see what's going on with Dwayne. I was trying to beat the traffic going to Atlanta. Luckily, it was before seven o'clock, so it wasn't that bad.

As I pulled up to his house, I noticed an unknown car parked in the driveway. I took my keys out of my pocketbook and shoved them in the door. My heart was beating fast, and my palms were sweaty. I know Dwayne never had company over, so for this car to be here, I thought it was a bitch that spent the night. The house was quiet; he had no idea I entered his home.

I nervously climbed the stairs in slow motion. I tried to tell myself I was overreacting. It could be a relative or his homeboy that spent the night. That was . . . right up to the point when I pushed his bedroom door open . . .

This nigga was laid up in the bed with a bitch. I cut the light on, walked over, and pulled the covers off them, exposing their naked asses. The nigga jumped up and looked at me like he had just seen a ghost.

"What the fuck you doin' in my house?" this bastard asked me.

"Who is this, babe, and what's she doing in your house?" the white meth-smoking bitch asked.

"Let me handle it, babe. She's an ex who had keys, and I forgot to change the locks."

"What the fuck you just said, nigga? An ex? Just a few days ago, I was your woman. Now you lying in bed wit' this cracker bitch?"

"Honey, I don't know what's going on, but I been his woman for two years."

"Bitch, shut up! I'm not yo' honey, and you couldn't be his woman. For the last two months, I've been spending every night here. This son of a bitch done sucked and licked my pussy and ate my ass every night."

My heart was pounding; I wanted to cry, but I wasn't going to let this fucked-up-ass nigga and bitch see me sweat.

"Sierra, that's enough. You up in my shit disrespecting my woman. You need to accept that we can never be." He got up out of bed and stepped toward me. I opened my purse and grabbed my gun.

"Don't you fucking come near me." I aimed it at him.

"Ha-ha. I see you a coward just like yo' son. Going around pulling guns on people but don't have the guts to use it. Bitch, get outta of my house before I call the cops and get yo' ass arrested for trespassing."

"Go on now, run along. Just because he fucked you a few times don't mean he wants your project ass. Shoot, I'm just mad he didn't let me watch," this ho said while smiling.

"You know what? Fuck you, nigga, and this dirty bitch. I bet you this ho wouldn't say this shit if you wasn't standing here. I fuckin' hate you," I said as I turned to walk away.

Everything in me was tellin' me to shoot that nigga and his ho, but I ain't no fool, and I wasn't going to risk my freedom behind that cheating-ass bastard.

I jumped in my car and pulled off. By the time I turned off the block, tears were pouring down my face. I couldn't get over that I believed this nigga, even though I knew niggas ain't no fucking good. This nigga had a bitch. Where the fuck her ass been for the last two months? You know what? Fuck this nigga. I can't believe that I cussed my son out behind his ass.

"Oh my God, what have I done?" I whispered.

I pulled up at the salon and sat in the car for a few minutes. I was mad as fuck, but I couldn't take that anger into work. I wiped my tears and got out of the car.

"Good morning, Boss Lady," Tanya said.

I didn't respond. I looked around to make sure none of the other workers or any customers were around; then I walked up to her.

"Tell me, Tanya, why didn't you tell me yo' brother had a girl?"

"Girl, what you talkin' 'bout?"

"Cut the fuckery out! Your snake ass knows what I'm talkin' 'bout," I snapped.

"Bitch, you mad or nah? You need to be going off on my brother; the last time I checked, he's the one fuckin' you, not me," this second-rate ho said.

"You grimy as fuck. You stayed in my face, bitch, and all along, you knew he was playin' me. What the fuck kind of woman are you?"

"Listen, that's my motherfuckin' brother, and I be damned if I was going to tell you his business when I don't know yo' ass from a can a paint. Bitch, please."

"You know, back in the day, I would've whupped yo' ass for being a no-good ass ho, but you ain't worth it. Bitch, get yo' shit and get out of my fuckin' shop."

"Bitch, I 'ont give a fuck 'bout this shit. You a mad bitch, 'cause you got played for a white bitch. I guess yo' pussy wasn't that good. Ha-ha, you is a fuckin' joke," she said, as she started packing up her things.

She didn't see it coming as she continued running her mouth. I punched that bitch in her face. She tried to grab me, but I pulled my gun on her.

"Bitch, leap if you want to, so I can blow your fucking head off."

She stopped dead in her tracks. She looked at me with her fist balled up and anger in her eyes.

"Bitch, that's all right. I'ma get yo' ass. You can't hide behind that gun forever."

"I told you before, I'm not your average bitch. I *will* kill you, ho. I put that on my seed. Now get out, before I throw you out." I walked over and opened the door so she could get the fuck on.

"Bitch, here go yo' keys." She threw them on the floor and sashayed out, cussing under her breath.

I locked the door and sat down. I needed a minute. I couldn't believe I'd just lost my temper like that. I knew better. These bitches be running their mouth but couldn't back it up. I knew I made a fucked-up move by hitting her ass. I can only hope she didn't press charges on me. Jail was not on my agenda.

I called the workers to let them know the shop was closed, and they could take the day off. Then I grabbed my bag, cut the lights off, and locked the door. I needed the day to gather my thoughts. I was still in shock.

"Sierra, is that you?" Jeanette yelled from the upstairs bedroom.

"Yeah, it's me. Who else could it be?"

"I thought you left for work."

"I did, but I'm not feeling well, so I decided to come back home," I lied.

"Oh, all right. You need some ginger tea?"

"No, I just want to lie down," I said, as I walked into my room and locked my door.

It was then that everything hit me in the face. Tears welled up in my eyes. All these fucking years I'd managed to stay away from niggas and their fucked-up ways. And here I was. I let my guard down with the wrong fucking nigga. I swear, while I was standing there I wanted to blow his fuckin' brains out. I wanted to hurt him the same way he stood there acting nonchalant like we hadn't made all these damn plans 'bout moving in together. The nigga even brought up marriage on numerous occasions. I lay across the bed and let it flow all out. Man, fuck these niggas; I swear I was tired of all of them. I see why bitches turn to other bitches. That's 'cause these niggas ain't shit. If all this nigga wanted was some pussy, shit, he could've said that. Shit, I was in need of some dick any motherfucking way.

I heard a knock at the door, which interrupted my thoughts.

"Who is it?" I hollered in an aggravated tone.

"It's me, Ma," Azir yelled.

"Give me a minute." I quickly wiped my tears and unlocked the door. "Come in."

He walked in, looking like his daddy. I couldn't help but smile at him.

"What's up, baby? I didn't know you was here."

"Nah. Just come through to check on y'all. Make sure e'eryting good."

"Oh, I see."

"Damn, Ma. You was crying?"

"Nah, I'm fine," I said. Who was I fooling? Tears were still rolling down.

"Ma, come here. What's going on?" He sat on the bed and put his arms around me. "Talk to me. What's going on wit' you? Did dat nigga hurt you? I ain't neva seen you cry before," he said angrily.

"Azir, I found out some foul shit 'bout him, that's all."

"Aye, Ma, I know we ain't been close or nothing, but trust me when I say dat nigga ain't nobody you tryin'a be wit'. This ain't on no hatin' shit. Me and that dude been had some words before. That's why I was tight when I walked in and seen y'all together."

"Azir, I didn't know nothin' 'bout y'all havin' words. Believe me, I would never bring a nigga in here if I knew my son had issues wit' him. Honestly, I thought you was on some jealousy kinda shit. I ain't know, baby." I cried in his arms.

"Don't trip, Ma. I ain't goin' lie. I went to see that nigga a few days ago, and he was talking recklessly out of the mouf. Straight callin' you all kind of bitches. I was seconds away from blowin' his head off. Nigga straight disrespected you in front of me, and I let him live, and now he got you over here crying and shit."

"Azir, don't you talk like that," I yelled. God, this boy done lost his mind, talkin' 'bout blowin' somebody head off. I didn't like this side of him. He reminded me of his daddy. His cockiness and anger . . .

"No, Ma, for real. This nigga better not hurt a hair on yo' head, and if he do, I'm going after him and his whole family."

"Azir, listen to me. I'm a big girl. I been around the block a few times. I can defend myself. Trust me, I 'ont go nowhere without 'Becky,' and believe me, I know how to use her."

"I feel you on that, but these dudes ain't to be played wit'. I know one thing fo' sure . . . If he want to stay breathin', he better stay away from mines."

He looked at me. I saw the same killer look in his eyes, just like his daddy had. I now knew he was no longer my innocent baby boy. He was now a man with deadly intentions!

"Forget all that. Tell me 'bout this new place." I tried to ease the tension in the air.

"It's cool. A three-bedroom condo in Conyers. Nothing fancy, just sump'n for me to lay my head at."

"Oh, okay, so you're renting it?"

"Nah, I bought it. You know I'm stacked up," he said jokingly.

"Okay, Mr. Big Money. I'm proud of you. That's a good move right there. Don't make sense wasting no money renting other people shit when you can own it. I'ma have to come see it one day."

"You already know it. You and Grandma should come over and cook me a li'l sump'n."

"Boy, no. You better ask one of yo' females. Oh, shoot, I forgot. Have you heard anything 'bout that girl that got killed?"

"Oh nah. I ain't tryin'a hear anything. Ma, me and her wasn't that serious. I fooled 'round wit' her a few times, so I ain't got no reason to keep up wit' her."

"Oh, okay, I would like to go to the funeral. I ain't really know her, outside of the few times you brought her to the house. It's really sad that she lost her life like that. I wonder what dude was wrapped up in."

"I 'ont know. Now I'm 'bout to go downstairs, but you sure you a'ight? Do I need to visit this nigga again?"

"Azir, I'm fine. Trust me. I need to know that you're going to leave this alone. Stay away from him. You hear me?" I looked him dead in the eyes.

"A'ight, Ma, I hear you. A'ight, let me know when you want to come over." He kissed me on the cheek.

I grabbed his arm. "Listen, I know I ain't been the best mom to you, but I need you to know I love you, and there's nothing in this world that I wouldn't do for you." I hugged him, and he left the room without saying a word.

I wish I could protect him, but I knew he was grown, and he made his own decisions now.

I got up, washed my face, and went downstairs. I could smell something good in the air. I knew Jeanette was throwing down in the kitchen again. I walked in to see her and Azir sitting down at the table, laughing and talking. I stood in the doorway smiling.

"What you standing there for? I made pancakes, sausage, eggs, and grits. Come make you a plate."

"Yeah, I'm starved. I like this; we haven't done this in a while. I love seeing my li'l family together. All we got is the three of us."

"A'ight, Ma, enough with all this emotional crap early in the morning," Azir laughed.

"OK, okay, Mr. Hard as a Rock. I'll stop showing my soft side," I played back.

"Hmm. I 'ont know what's goin' on, but I think God answered my prayer. I prayed for this day to come, and look at this; we are sittin' here like a family, laughing and talkin'. I tell you 'bout the power of my God."

Both Azir and I looked at each other. We knew once she started preaching, she wouldn't stop. *Lord help us,* I thought!

Azir Jackson

"I need a vacation. I'm goin' to Decatur where it's greater. See if I could stack me up some more paper. . . ." Jeezy's voice blasted through the speakers.

I was on my way to Mom-duke's crib. I decided it was time that I cleaned my clothes out of the room. Shit, I had so many outfits, I could donate some.

Jeezy's song had me in the zone. Lately, shit ain't been going right. I didn't know how long I was gonna stick around. If e'erything worked out as planned, I would be closing shop and movin' on. I ain't no fool; if my name kept ringing bells, it'd only be a matter of time before Babylon started paying attention. I ain't never been locked up before, and I wanted to keep it that way. Don't get me wrong. I knew I was living foul, and if I have to lay a nigga down, I will—'cause at the end of the day, I rather be judged by twelve than carried by six. Real nigga talk.

I parked my Jeep in the driveway and walked to the door. The house was quiet, so I was hoping Mom-dukes wasn't home. I had too much on my brain right now, and I didn't want to get into it with her. I wish sometimes we could have a real mother-and-son bond, but that's all it was. A wish.

I walked past her bedroom, then took a few steps back. I leaned my ear against the door and heard sobbing sounds. I immediately banged on the door.

She told me to come in, so I opened the door. There she was, lying in bed. She tried her best to hide her tears, but I could see. Her eyes were puffy, and her voice was hoarse.

I wasted no time trying to find out what was going on, and she tried her best to keep the truth away from me. She saw that I wasn't letting up, so she finally broke down, telling me that the pussyclaat nigga she was messing around with was the reason why she was crying.

Every second this nigga continued to breathe, he found a way to make my life hell. There was no way 'round it; I needed to handle him ASAP.

It hurt my soul to see my moms crying like that. I knew whatever it was this nigga did, it was serious. I held her tight as she bawled in my arms. This shit was blowing me to see her sitting up, crying over this bum-ass nigga that she had no business fucking wit' in the first place.

I sat and kicked it wit' her for a minute. This was the first time that we actually sat down and had a grown-up conversation without yelling. I ain't goin' lie; it felt kind of good. She was a cool person when she ain't got all that attitude and shit. I ended up tellin' her 'bout how that fuck nigga called her out of her name. I didn't hold back anything and even went as far as letting her know that I wanted to kill that nigga. I saw the surprised look that she gave me. See, she's never really seen me in action, which was good, 'cause as soon as things pop off, the first person Babylon run to is the mother. I would never want to put or jeopardize her freedom behind some shit that I did.

I was a man on a mission! I put on my all-black Dickies outfit and black Nike boots. I decided to ride out on my latest toy, a Kawasaki Ninja Zx-14.

I put on my helmet with the mirror-tinted visor and pulled off. It took me no time to get to the spot. I parked my bike in the alley behind the coffee shop and walked around the side of the building so I could watch this chump handling business. It was a little past nine o'clock when I noticed the assistant leaving. I knew then he would be following shortly. I jumped on my bike and pulled to the side just in time to see him pull off in his dark-colored Dodge Charger. I eased out in traffic without raising suspicion and followed closely, careful not to speed.

I thought it was crazy how these niggas be in the streets but didn't have no street sense. The nigga didn't notice that a bike followed him from Decatur all the way to Atlanta. Talk 'bout dumb-ass niggas. I watched closely as he pulled into a driveway and got out of the car. Then I sped up close enough to the driveway, and as I pulled my pistol out, I saw the look of shock on his face as he noticed what was 'bout to take place.

Bop! Bop! Bop! Shots rang out. He fell to the ground, and I jumped off the bike, ran up on him, and emptied the clip in his face.

"Dead yuh fi dead pussyhole," I said as I ran back to my bike and burned tires. In seconds, I was ghost and got the hell out of Atlanta.

I made it back to Decatur and pulled over in an empty parking lot. I pulled the gun apart and threw it in the woods behind an abandoned building. I kept the barrel so I could take it to the scrap yard. After that, I stopped by the store and grabbed me a pack of Dutches. I made it to the house and circled the block three times before I rode into my subdivision.

Whoo! What a day, I thought.

Walking in, I went directly to the bar and poured me a glass of Jamaican White Rum, no water or ice. I took it straight to the dome. Then I rolled me a big head and poured another glass of rum before I walked into the living room.

This shit felt good as fuck. I got another killin' under my belt. The only difference, this one was close to my heart. This pussyclaat nigga violated me, but more importantly, he violated my moms. I bet that pussy ain't laughing right now! Betta yet, that nigga's lights went out for good.

I barely even watched my 50-inch plasma TV, but I needed to see what the news people were reporting. Channel 2 had breaking news: A murder in an upper-class neighborhood in the Buckhead area. There were lots of police cars, news people, and nosy neighbors. The news reporter stated that Atlanta PD believed that this was drug-related since the victim was a known drug dealer and gangbanger. I watched as the reporter pointed to the medical examiner roll the corpse. I cut my TV off and took a few more pulls out of this ganja I was smoking. Relaxing with my blunt, liquor, and Bob Marley chanting in the background, I sat back on the sofa.

Today was a good day if I do say so myself . . . "This is for you, Pops." I raised my glass to salute the man that I'd never met.

Chapter Eleven

Shayna Jackson

"Hello, Miss Jackson. I'm Superintendent Beckenham, and this is Investigator Clarkston from the Bureau of Prison Headquarters. Sit down."

"Hello." I took a seat across from the two big burly officers.

Hmm, this is some serious shit, I thought. I straightened myself up and put on my game face. I was on alert. Had to make sure I was on point; I didn't trust these crackers. I already knew they were trying to cover their asses, especially after the news carried it the other day. That shit didn't look good. "*Federal inmate raped while in custody.*" My lawyer must smell money, 'cause this fool been talking to everybody who would listen.

"All right, Miss Jackson, I know you've told the story before, but I need you to tell it to us again."

"Really? I wrote a statement. Shouldn't that be enough? I even gave up his semen. You don't believe me, do you?" I busted out crying.

"No, that's not what I'm implying. I'm sorry if you feel like that. You're a victim and deserve justice. This should never happen to any woman." This racist-ass slave master looked straight at me and lied, right to my face.

I didn't pay him any mind. I started to tell them my story from beginning to end, without blinking. They had no idea who they were fucking with. My freedom depended on this; there was no way I was going to mess that up. By the time I was finished, both of them were sitting there with pity plastered across their faces. The superintendent even looked like he had tears in his eyes. *What a fucking fool,* I thought.

"Okay, Mrs. Jackson, my office is doing a thorough investigation. The officer will have no contact with you. Your lawyer is in contact with my office. I do give you my sincere apologies that this happened to you. I promise you that you will be given justice," the BOP idiot said.

"Thank you so much. I can't sleep, can't eat. Nothing like this has ever happened to me before. I thought I was safe here, but this happened. He threatened me; he told me that if I tell, y'all wouldn't believe me and would give me more time."

"Don't you worry 'bout a thing. My office is handling everything. I'm going to make sure you never have to experience this again. You're free to go. I'll be contacting your lawyer."

"Okay. Thank you, gentlemen, so much. I'm glad someone believes me," I bawled.

"Okay, Mrs. Jackson." He opened the door for me. I saw in his eyes that he was ready for me to get the fuck on.

I pranced out of the office, still wiping tears in case they were watching me from the office window.

Oh Lord, that was a task, but I got it done. I was feeling confident that things would work out in my favor. Shit, I didn't really lie; I am a federal inmate, which meant I had no rights, so I couldn't consent to sleep with him. So, technically, in a court of law, he raped me.

I walked back to the unit and saw a bunch of low-life hood rats standing at the door; the minute they saw me, they started to whisper. I walked past them and looked them dead in their eyes. I saw the fear as they turned their heads.

I walked into the unit and headed straight to the phone, where I dialed my lawyer's number.

"Miss Jackson, how are you doing today?"

"I'm terrible. Can't sleep at nights. Can't stop crying. The superintendent and some man from BOP came to see me today," I cried.

"Okay. That's great. I'm sure they just wanted you to go over what happened. I filed a motion on your behalf for immediate release. So sit tight, I'm working every angle, not leaving any stone unturned."

I could've hugged him! Shit, I probably would've sucked this fool's cock right now. That's the kind of news that I was waiting to hear. God knows I was tired of this hellhole. I was ready to go and get back to my life.

"Okay, thank you. I do appreciate you being there for me."

"Take care of yourself. Let me work on the legal side. Give me a call next week, 'cause I'm pushing for immediate release." Those were the last words I heard before the phone cut off.

I walked out of the phone booth, smiling ear to ear.

"You evil bitch. I knew that it was some shit wit' you. Gonzalez is a good officer; he treated us better than anybody else. You know damn well that man didn't rape you. You threw yourself on him. I watched you, bitch. You got everybody 'round here fooled, except me. Bitch, I can see through your lies," this Big Bertha bitch yelled as she hovered over me.

I almost snapped on this ho, but I quickly remembered I have too much to lose.

"Listen up, bitch. Mind your own business and stay out of mine. You don't know what Gonzalez did to me. I might've flirted with him, but that didn't give him the right to rape me. You're a woman and should understand how I'm feeling."

"Bitch, I don't believe you. You come in here acting like you better than us—well, I have news for you. Your shit stink just like the rest of us. Look around you; you have an eight-digit number, and you are in khakis just like the rest of us. Bitch, you just a common ho, tryin'a pretend like you high class. Too bad Gonzalez didn't see you for the rotten snake that you really are."

"Listen, you crackhead bitch; I tried to be nice to yo' slow ass. I'm done being nice to you. Run the fuck along, find some pussy to suck on, and get the fuck out of my way." I pushed her ass out of my way.

The nerve of this bitch. She called her ass trying to check me over a police-ass nigga. That big bitch betta continue pressing her bunk and stay the fuck up outta my way. I'm definitely not what she wanted.

I walked to my bunk because it was almost count time. I was so caught up in everything going on that I'd forgotten to eat. I opened my locker and grabbed a cup of noodles. Oh, I was so tired of eating that shit. Before prison, I thought that shit was all them project bitches ate. *Oh well, it won't be much longer,* I thought.

"Hey, Miss Shayna, you 'ont happen to have another one of those to spare?"

"Chantelle, aren't you tired of begging? Damn, bitch, you need a hustle or something," I said, slammed my locker, and walked off. That poor bitch stayed begging for soap to wash her ass or noodles. Fuck, I was tired of her ass. I was ready to go!

Over the next couple of days, I spoke to Alonzo over the phone. I don't know what it was about this man, but I couldn't seem to get him off my mind. His words were so soothing, and he seemed so different from all the other lames that tried to get with me. His in-control attitude turned me on. I swear I thought it was Alijah reincarnated.

"Ha-ha, bitch, you trippin'," I said to myself. Alijah's ass was dead and buried in some hole in Jamaica. They lucky I wasn't home, because I'm the wife; I would've burned his fucking body. That fucked-up-ass nigga took my daddy away from me. I should've killed his little monkey when I had the chance. Speaking of him, I wonder whatever happened to him. He should be around twenty or twenty-one, the same amount of time I've been in here. Hmm, his ass might be up in somebody's jail if he was anything like his daddy. I can't wait 'til I get out of here. I got plans . . . *big* plans.

Chapter Twelve

Shayna Jackson

"Shayna Jackson to visitation."

"Shayna, that's you, girl. You might have good news."

"You just don't get it, do you? Mind your own fucking business, bitch," I yelled at my nosy-ass bunkie.

I got off my bunk, put my sneakers on, and strolled off to the R&D. *I hope this is it,* I thought.

"Come in, Miss Jackson," Lieutenant Hernandez said.

I stepped into the office and noticed Superintendent Beckenham standing there.

"Hello, again, Miss Jackson. Sit down." He pointed to the seat.

What's going on here? I thought.

"In our last meeting, I told you I was going to get to the bottom of what happened to you. I had my team investigate, and no stones were left unturned. That led me to the conclusion that Officer Gonzalez did violate you; I want to give you my sincere apology, and I promise you, he will be arrested and get his day in court to answer to this heinous crime against you."

"Oh my God. I thought he would not be arrested for what he did," I busted out crying.

"Well, Miss Jackson, after all you've been through, I spoke to the Bureau of Prisons. Your lawyer and I are pushing for immediate release."

I froze in my seat. Did this cracker say *immediate release?* I wanted to jump up and down, but I knew I couldn't. I had to continue acting as if I was a victim.

"Your release papers are submitted; we are waiting for the judge to sign off on them, which could be any day."

I was at a loss for words; I continued crying. They thought I was crying because I was victimized. Hell nah! I was crying because in a few days or weeks, I knew I'd be walking out of this hellhole. I knew the judge would see fit to send me home. The case was already shedding a negative light on the federal government and the Bureau of Prisons.

"I think we are finished here. You will hear from us in a few days. In the meantime, your counselor will be discussing your terms of release with you."

"Thank you," I managed to mumble through all the crying that I was doing.

I walked out of the office and headed toward the track. I needed a minute to gather my thoughts. Shit, I've wasted all these years; I wish that I had thought about this a long time ago. All kinds of emotions filled my mind . . . the thought of being able to walk the streets again. I smiled as I sniffed the fresh air. Oh, I couldn't wait to be able to sleep in my own bed and do what the fuck I wanted to do.

"Sierra Rogers, get ready! The game is not over until *I* say so," I said under my breath. There was not one day that I was in here that I haven't thought about her and that li'l monkey. This bitch was the sole reason that I was locked up. Ever since that bitch walked into my life, all she did was create havoc. I was disappointed when I learned she wasn't dead. What the fuck? That bitch must have nine lives; I shot her close range last time, and I thought I killed her, only to find out her old ghetto ass lived. I thought of us meeting again. I won't rest until that bitch is in the ground, where the fuck she belongs. I was so engulfed in my thoughts that I didn't notice the rain was coming down until I was soaked! I got into the unit and took a quick shower before count time.

After dinner, I decided to make a phone call to Alonzo. For the past month, we have grown closer. This fool had no idea that he was just another fool. For the time being, he served a purpose, even though I found myself thinking about him when I went to bed and when I woke up.

I dialed his number and waited until the recording did its thing.

"Hello, love?"

"Hey, you. I am so happy right now. Can you guess what just happened?"

"I ain't wit' no guessing, but I figure it's good news 'cause of how you acting."

"Yes. I'll be home in a little while. Home? Wait, I have no home. Ha-ha," I laughed nervously.

"Word! You're finished? I thought you had 'bout three years left."

"Well, I did, but it's a long story that I will have to tell you in person if we ever meet." I wasn't no fool. I knew all the conversations were recorded.

"Oh, a'ight. So, you going back to New York?"

"Damn! I haven't thought about it yet. Uh, I have to figure it out soon, though."

"Shit, you need to come out here wit' a nigga. I mean, starting over might be all you need."

"You mean, out in Atlanta? I never been there before."

"Shit, I mean—you might as well move out here wit' me. I got you!"

"Hmm. I sense someone is inviting me to his domain."

"I got the space, and if you don't feel comfortable, I can pull some strings and get you your own place."

"Wow! I don't know what to say. I don't really know you, and I wouldn't want to impose on your life."

"Listen up, ma, I'm the one that offered. Cut the bullshit out. The offer is open. Get at a nigga when you make yo' decision."

Before I could respond, the phone hung up. I wasn't sure if he hung up or the phone cut off. I was shocked that he asked me to come out there with him. Atlanta, huh? I've never been there, but I've heard great things about the city. It might not be a bad idea. It ain't like I had anyone in New York. Daddy was gone and going back to Long Island would only bring back memories of his horrible death. I had enough money from Daddy's estate that would allow me to live comfortably. I knew that I could never practice law again. Oh well, let's see what I can get into when I hit Hotlanta, as everyone calls it.

I walked back to my bunk thinking; I have some planning to do . . .

Chapter Thirteen

Sierra Rogers

I hate to question God, but why did I have such bad luck with men? First, Alijah got killed, and now Dwayne. Damn, even though he and I broke up, and he did me wrong, it didn't make the pain any less. I had so many great memories of us together.

His sister had called me, even though we got into it the other day. I didn't fuck wit' that bitch like that, and the only reason why I talked to her ass was because his mother was also on the phone. That bitch was a straight up snake that I needed to stay away from. She had the nerve to ask me for some money to put toward his funeral. Hell nah! This nigga was one of Atlanta's biggest dope boys. You mean to tell me, they had to call li'l ole me for money? Hell, they better call that cracker bitch. It's *her* man and *her* responsibility, and if they couldn't afford a funeral, they needed to cremate his ass. The bitch had an attitude when I told her poor ass that I wasn't gonna help. That's when I became a "stupid bitch" again. I didn't give a fuck what that ho called me; I bet she couldn't call me a broke bitch!

I haven't talked to Mo' in a while. I sure miss my bitch. She's supposed to visit next month. I can't wait. Even though I didn't know Atlanta that well, there was a lot of shit to do out here. I've heard a lot about Magic City and the infamous Blue Flame, two of the hottest strip clubs in Atlanta. I know Mo's ass would be in heaven. Also, there's a few food places that a few of my clients be bragging out. We will definitely find something to get into.

I dialed Mo's number.

"Hey, chica."

"Hey, boo. What's going on?"

"Nothing, just sitting here missin' yo' ass, so I decided to hit you up."

"Oh, okay. I'm sitting here filling out this application for my new place."

"Word? You're moving?"

"Yes, girl, I'm tired of Richmond. These niggas and all these killings is really blowin' me. I'm trying to move out to Chesterfield, where it's quiet, and all the hoodlums won't be out there. You know Chesterfield police don't be playing."

"Yeah, I feel you on that. Girl, you remember ole boy that I told you 'bout when we were talkin'?"

"Yeah, I remember. The one that wanted y'all to move in. What's going on wit' y'all?"

"Girl, that nigga was a fucking cheater. I caught him in bed with a white bitch. Come to find out, she was his woman. I was the fuckin' sidepiece. Anyway, girl, somebody killed him a few nights ago."

"Bitch, you lying? For what?"

"I have no idea. He was a big-time dope boy, or so it seemed."

"Yo, that's fucked up. How you holding up? I know he cheated and all, but you had a relationship with him."

"Girl, I ain't goin' lie. It hurts, but I think I'm still angry that his ass played me like that. After what I've been through wit' Alijah, I didn't expect to get dogged out like this."

"Girl, these niggas ain't shit. You know that. But on some real shit, friend, I believe yo' pussy is deadly. That's the second nigga you fucked that end up dead. Damn! But I got the pussy too. Does that mean that I'm next?" She busted out laughing.

"Fuck you, Mo', wit' yo' retarded ass. Ain't shit wrong wit' my pussy. These niggas just not getting it. The street don't love them. I do feel bad for his seed and his mama. Girl, me and his trifling-ass sister got into it the other day. That bitch two-faced. She knew her brother had a bitch. I smacked the shit out of her, trying to disrespect me when I confronted her."

"Really? This country bitch betta stay in her fuckin' lane, 'cause I'll be headin' down 95 South if she keep fuckin' wit' you."

"Bitch, you know I handled that ho; she wasn't ready. The younger me would've beat her to death, but my old ass ain't trying to sit up in nobody jail cell eating bologna sandwiches. I fired that bitch on the spot. I was not playing."

"These bitches betta get their shit in order, 'cause I ain't nothing but eight hours away."

"Okay, Ms. Laila Ali. They ain't ready for you." We both laughed.

"Anyway, what going on wit' you?"

"Girl, nothing. Same shit, different day. Just been workin' my ass off."

Jeanette walked into the room and interrupted. "Sierra, cut the TV on."

"I'm on the phone. What is it?" I asked with an attitude.

"The news is on; it's showing a commercial now, but it's coming up next," she said as she cut on the television.

"Mo', let me hit you back later."

"Okay, cool." She hung up the phone.

"Jeanette, what's so important that you had to interrupt me?"

Before she could respond, the Channel 2 news reporter came on. *"Yes, Julia, I just finished talking to Atlanta PD, and they confirmed to me what we've heard all morning. A motorcycle was involved in the shooting death of Dwayne McKenzie. One witness that was out walking her dog told investigators that around 9:15 p.m. while out, she heard gunshots and hid behind a car. She caught a glimpse of a big motorcycle speeding away from the scene of the crime. She wasn't able to see the rider's face, because he was wearing a helmet and wore black clothing. The police are withholding this witness's name because the investigators are still gathering evidence. The FBI is also involved in this case because the victim was under federal investigation. Ross Colbert reporting from Atlanta for Channel 2 News. Jovita, back to you."*

I sat frozen in my seat. I looked over at Jeanette, and I knew our thoughts were similar.

"No, this is pure coincidence." I shook my head in disbelief. "I spoke to him earlier, and he said he didn't have anything to do with the killing. I believe him," I told her.

She didn't respond. She sat there humming to herself. I got up and headed upstairs.

I lay across my bed thinking, and my thoughts wandered back to the last time Azir was here. How angry he was that dude did me wrong. I remember hearing the anger in his voice and seeing the coldness in his eyes; it sent chills up my spine just thinking about it. Oh no! I hope that I didn't drive my baby to commit murder.

"Oh my God. Please protect my only child. I can't take it. I just can't . . ." I cried out to God. I hope it was all a coincidence. My baby ain't no killer! My mind was tellin' me one thing, but my heart was telling me different. Azir was so much like his dad, and that's the part that was trying to tell me different . . .

Chapter Fourteen

Shayna Jackson

It was 1:00 a.m., and I couldn't fall asleep; maybe it was anxiety. I lay on my bunk looking up at the dark ceiling. Less than eight hours, I'd be walking out of these walls and into the real world. The real world—I *love* the sound of that. After spending all these fucking years in hell, I'd be able to eat, shit, and sleep when I want to, without worrying about these motherfuckers breathing down my back.

I was looking forward to starting a new chapter in my life. I've got all that money from Daddy's estate and my money I had stashed away overseas. If I must say so, I was going home to be one rich bitch! And I've got a new man in my life. Well, let's not jump to conclusions there. I plan to see what's up with this fool. I needed to find out how much paper he was stacking, then figure out a way to get mine out of it, and then get the hell on.

After tying up some loose ends, I think I might move to an exotic island, with blue water and men with tan bodies and big muscles. That's the life right there, I thought as I dozed off.

I jumped up when this loud-ass bitch hollered, "Work time," over the intercom. Damn, it's already 7:00 a.m. I jumped off my bunk, grabbed my clothes, and headed for the shower room. I showered and got dressed in no time. The hairstylist in the bootleg beauty shop flat ironed my hair, which was below my ass. I applied a little makeup. Since this was the cheap version, I was careful not to put on too much. Damn sure didn't want my face to break out. I put on my grey jogging suit. I couldn't wait to get to Atlanta so that I could hit the designer stores up. They thought I was conceited before. They ain't seen shit. Those Atlanta bitches better watch and take notes from a *real* diva.

I handed all the clothes and things that I'd accumulated all these years to the Spanish bitch that did my hair.

I saw the anger in my bunkie's eyes. I didn't pay her ass any mind. If she had any doubt that I didn't like her ass, she should be certain now. That bitch snored, coughed, farted, and begged every chance she got. Old disgusting-ass bitch.

"Shayna Jackson, to R&D."

"That's you, Miss Shayna. You go, girl; make sure you keep in touch."

"Bitch, get outta my way." I pushed past her.

I walked out unit 3-C, held my head high, and walked across the compound. As I walked past a few inmates, I saw the jealousy in their eyes. They wished that it was them leaving. Oh well, let them bitches keep wishing. After all, I didn't sit back and wish. I took my destiny in my own hands . . .

The plane ride from Florida to Atlanta was only an hour and twenty minutes, so in no time, I was walking out of the airport. I was also feeling nervous. I kept looking all around me and would jump when someone got close to me. I kept coaching myself to calm down as I walked through this gigantic airport. As I got closer to where people would pick up visitors, I started to feel nauseated. What was I doing? Maybe I should turn around and buy another ticket and head to New York. Right as that thought entered my mind, I saw a dude walking toward me. Our eyes locked. I recognized that it was the same dude that was in the pictures.

"Shayna, right?" I heard a seductive voice say; it almost sounded like Barry White.

I stopped and stared rudely before saying anything. In front of me was every woman's fantasy. A tall, brown-skinned, long dreads brother stood before me. To say he was fine would be an understatement. Those eyes, though, were dark, cold, and deadly.

"Well, hello, there," I managed to say in a low tone.

"Well, come here, woman. I'm Lonzo," he said, pulling me toward him and hugging me.

He smelled so good I almost collapsed in his arms. I wasn't sure what he was wearing, but whatever it was triggered my hormones.

"You ready?"

"Yes! I'm more than ready. I'm starved, and I need to go shopping."

"I understand that. I'm parked this way. Let's go."

Lord, I don't know this man, and here I was in his state with him. *I hope he ain't no killer or rapist,* I thought as we walked to his truck.

The rest of the evening was spent shopping at the luxurious stores in Buckhead, which was considered the wealthy area of Atlanta. I stood in awe as we entered the mall. Things just look so different than when I was home. I became overwhelmed. People were moving all around me, which made me nervous. I thought about turning around and running back to the truck, but I know this is something that I had to deal with. No one warned me that after being this long from the streets, so much would've changed.

"Yo, you good?" he tapped me on the arm.

"Yes, I just feel crazy being in a store after all these years."

"Do you want to leave? We can come back another day, or you can shop online."

"No, I can't stay locked in forever. We're here, so I'm ready to hit these stores."

This damn mall was huge, and it has some of my favorite stores and a lot of new ones that I've never heard of before. This nigga was definitely a big-time baller. Store after store, he kept pulling out wads of cash. I was fine with it, because he spent almost ten grand on me—from designer pants to dresses and purses. Then I hit up Victoria's Secret so that I could get some fancy underwear and lingerie. This nigga was spending like that, so I had no problem fucking and sucking him off. I knew that if I played my cards right, it wouldn't be long before I'd be deep down in his pockets.

Finally, he pulled up at his house; it was a nice condo. Nothing big; just cozy enough to feel like home. I glanced around as we entered; it was very clean and masculine.

"Make yo'self at home. We can share a bedroom, or you can have yo' own room. The choice is yours, pretty lady."

"I like the sound of that. We can share a room. I don't think you gonna bite me, and if you did, I'd just have to bite yo' ass back," I joked.

"Ha-ha. I see you're also a comedian."

He had no idea how serious I was about that statement. If he continued to play his cards right, he'd have no reason to find out how hard I could bite, but if I found out this nigga was on any kind of bullshit, he'd feel the wrath of Miss Shayna Jackson!

Azir Jackson

I'd spent my entire life dreaming about meeting the person that betrayed my pops and tried to kill my moms. I remember going to bed e'ery night and planning on how I was going to get to them. Even though I'd never met that bitch, I used to hear my nana whispering about this woman, and after reading the newspaper clippings, I had nothing but hatred in my heart for her. I knew that as long as I had life, one day we would meet.

I'd seen her face in the old newspaper clippings that I took from underneath Nana's bed, but it wasn't until Natasha showed me the most recent pictures of her that I was able to stare in the eyes of this evil bitch.

Fast-forward to this minute; only Jah knows how much I'd prayed for this day. I stood in the lobby of the airport waiting to pick her up. Everything was working out the way I planned it. I peeped as she walked out and looked around. This bitch had no idea that she was entering the world of a man that was seeking revenge for his family. I walked up on her and said her name. I knew I startled her by the way she jumped. This old bitch stood in front of me with her tongue hanging out of her mouth as if she were a fucking hungry dog. I played it cool, though. I was a patient man; I've waited all these years, so waiting a few more days was minor.

I ended up taking her shopping. Yeah, I dropped a couple of Gs on that greedy bitch. Watched as her face lit up when I pulled out a stack of hundreds. It was my way of reeling her in so she would have no doubt that I was a boss; exactly the kind of niggas she was attracted to.

Chapter Fifteen

Shayna Jackson

After we ate dinner, he opened a bottle of Cîroc Pineapple. This was new to me, but once I tasted it, it immediately won me over. We laughed and talked as if we'd known each other for a lifetime. He was a laid-back man; that made me feel comfortable around him.

"Well, it's getting late. I'm about to shower and slip into something a bit more comfortable," I winked at him.

Damn! I had to get into the shower. I was sitting there looking at his sexy body and listening to his sultry voice, and it made my pussy juice overflow through my cheap-ass prison drawers.

I got into the shower and carefully washed every inch of my voluptuous body. This Dove Body Wash was doing the body well. I used the washcloth and scrubbed hard, with the intent to wash that filthy place off me. It was a new start and all new beginnings.

I stepped out of the shower leaving all the dirt of my old life behind me. This was the new and improved Miss Jackson.

Next, I grabbed the oil I bought from Victoria's Secret earlier and gently oiled my body. I rubbed across my breasts, my thighs, and between my legs. I stuck my finger into my pussy and licked it. I loved the taste of sweet nectar; it sent my sex drive up to an all-time high. I was ready for whatever awaited me on the other side of the door—or was I?

Slowly, I opened the door and took one step forward. I looked at his face . . . then down to his cock! Around nine inches of beautifully well-endowed chocolate manhood stood in front of me, and it was thick as hell, making this one of the most beautiful cocks I have ever seen in my life, and trust me, I've seen a variety of cocks.

"Don't just stand there looking at the mother-fucker. Come show him some love."

I was happy he interrupted my thoughts 'cause my mouth was gathering water. I wanted to lick that cock and satisfy my sexual appetite.

I dropped the towel and stepped closer to him. He picked me up and put me in the air, then buried his head in my pussy. My clit throbbed as he licked in a circular pattern. I couldn't take it; my legs started to shake as I exploded in his mouth.

He didn't loosen up any and continued to suck on my clit aggressively, which sent me into a multiple-orgasm frenzy. My body trembled, my chest tightened, and I held his head tight. Pussy juice flowed out freely all over his beard. He then carried me to the bed and entered me from the back. My pussy was wet and welcomed his overgrown cock without any restrictions. He started off slowly but soon picked up speed. He fucked me like he was on a mission. I tried to throw my ass back at him, but the pressure prevented me from moving. I buried my face in one of the pillows and bit down hard. I've been fucked before, but it was nothing compared to this. This was the kind of cock that will have you losing your mind. Damn! I wouldn't mind getting my pussy serviced every night if it was gonna be like this!

After 'bout two hours of fucking and sucking in every room, on the bed, on the carpet, and even on the kitchen counter, we were both exhausted. I took a quick washup and crawled into bed. He soon followed. He held me in his strong arms as I dozed off thinking this man could be my Prince Charming if he played his cards right. This meant he had to eat my pussy good, fuck me good, and made sure I had all the money I needed. And most importantly, he had to stay away from those low-level hoes. If he did all that, we surely could have a future together.

I woke up the next morning hoping it wasn't a dream, and sure enough, it wasn't. Across from me lay my man; I also noticed a firearm on the nightstand on his side of the bed. That reminded me that I needed to find one ASAP. Yeah yeah yeah, I'm a convicted felon, so I'm not supposed to carry a firearm. Bullshit! The feds fucked up my life. There was no way I was gonna let them still run my life. I'd paid my dues and some more. Shit, they owed *me,* if you want to be technical about it.

"Good morning, beautiful." He looked at me and smiled.

"Hmm, somebody was tired, 'cause you sure was snorin' heavily," I teased.

"Cut it out. A nigga ain't doing no snoring." He threw the pillow at me.

"Uh-huh. So you say." I threw the pillow back at him.

"So, Alonzo, how is your cousin doing? I would love to see her. That was my girl."

"I ain't talked to her in a minute, but I'm pretty sure she good. I'ma let her know you in town. Y'all should get up with each other."

"I'm just trying to adjust to life on the outside. A lot has changed."

"Yeah, it'll take some time, but you good. Before you know it, you'll forget about prison."

"No, I'll never forget. I hated that place with a passion."

"Let me ask you a quick question. What did a pretty lady like yo'self do to land you in the feds?"

"Hmm . . . long story. I tried to kill this bitch that made my life hell."

"Hell nah. Not you. You 'ont look like you could hurt a fly," he laughed.

I caught an instant attitude. He was laughing like it was a joke. That bitch Sierra entered my life and fucked it up. My soul wouldn't rest until that bitch took her final breath.

"Yo, you a'ight?" I felt him shaking me.

"Yes, I'm fine. Sorry 'bout that. It was a traumatic time in my life, and it hurts every time I think about it," I said.

"I understand, ma. I didn't mean to hurt you or anything like that. We don't have to talk 'bout it until you're ready."

"I'm fine. I'm a big girl."

"Listen, all this is behind you now. You're here with me, and I ain't goin' do nothing to hurt you. That's on e'erything I love."

Damn, this nigga catching feelings already with all this emotional shit. Shit, I hope I didn't have another Markus on my hands. Sadness overcame me with the thought of Markus. The last time I heard, they still haven't found him or his body, and Alijah was dead, so there's little or no hope that he'd ever be found. It's sad that he just vanished like that. I quickly snapped back to reality. Markus was the past; I'm on to bigger fish!

"Alonzo, you have an accent; sounds like Jamaican or Trinidadian."

"Yeah, my father was from Jamaica, and I spent a few years out there when I was a kid. I didn't realize that it was that strong."

"No, it's not really strong; I just picked up on it, because my husband was from there, and I visited a few times myself."

"Word! You were married?"

"Yes, I was, but unfortunately, he was killed 'bout a year before I went to prison."

"Damn! Sorry fo' yo' loss. That must be rough and all. You one strong woman."

"Nothing to be sorry 'bout. The bastard left me for a younger project bitch. I wasn't really sad when his ass got killed. He had put me through too much. Cheating, calling me all kind of bitches, even went as far as hitting me. Then came the ultimate disrespect. He got the little bitch he was sleeping with pregnant. The bitch ended up having the little bastard."

"Damn, that nigga did you like that? Some niggas don't appreciate a good woman. He got everything he deserved if he did you like that."

"Yeah, he wasn't worth shit but some money. The bastard was paid, and that's the only reason I stuck around long as I did."

"Well, I'm glad he fucked up 'cause if he didn't, you wouldn't be here right now. Trust me; I ain't nothin' like that nigga."

Yeah, right. All these bums have the same line when they first get in a relationship. I didn't bother to say anything. I just looked at him and smiled. This was weird, his face . . . He reminds me of someone. Hmm, I know. He reminds me of Alijah. I chuckled to myself. Here I am claiming that I didn't care 'bout his death, but I thought Alonzo reminded me of him. My mind was playing tricks on me. I brushed that craziness off 'cause Alijah was an only child, and he had a son, who last I heard was living in Jamaica with his grandma. That was years and years ago. Something rang an alarm in my head, but this can't be. I brushed off the feeling as my mind was only playing tricks on me.

"You a'ight? You actin' a little strange," he inquired.

"I'm fine. So what are yo' plans for today?" I asked, trying to brush away my thoughts.

"'Bout to get up. Got to handle some business in Atlanta; then I plan on spending the rest of the day with you."

"Oh, okay. Sounds great. I need to make some phone calls, so I'm going to relax until you get back in."

I took my shower and made us a light breakfast. He didn't have a lot of food in the refrigerator, so I made scrambled eggs, grits, and toast.

We sat at the table, eating, talking, and looking into each other's eyes. *This seems so real,* I thought.

"A'ight, babe, I'm out. Make yo'self at home."

I watched as he pulled out of the driveway. *Okay, I'm free,* I thought. I made sure the doors were locked; then I pranced upstairs. I took out the envelope that contained everything about my case and stuck it in the bottom of the drawer where my clothes were folded. Then my nosy behind started going through his drawers. I couldn't help but wonder what he was hiding. We all have secrets, even if it's nothing major. I searched through his clothes, through papers, and under the bed, but had no luck finding anything of importance. Okay, now, since that was out of the way, I had some phone calls to make. First, I called Wells Fargo to request a new bank card. I then called Nova Scotia Bank in the

Cayman Islands to check on my money. The next call was to Daddy's lawyer. I had to inform him that I was going to sell the house in Hempstead and the vacation home up in Massachusetts. I didn't want to keep anything that would remind me of Daddy.

I found a phone book in his kitchen and decided to look up a private investigator. I found one in Marietta, Georgia. I had no idea how far it was from me, but it stated that he's been in the business for over thirty years, and he was the best in the business. Let's see how good he was. I dialed the number that was listed.

"Hello, Richardson here," a groggy voice said.

"Good morning. I'm calling because I saw an ad in the Yellow Pages and I'm in need of a PI."

"Well, here I am at your service, ma'am. What is it exactly you need my help with?"

"Well, I would love to meet with you in person and discuss the case. I need to have someone that I can trust."

"Sure. I understand. What side of town are you on?"

"I believe it's Decatur."

"All right. We can meet in Atlanta, which would be the closest to both of us."

"Yeah, that's fine. I'm not from the area, so I would have to figure it out. Thursday is good for me. What about you?"

"Let me see something . . . Yeah, Thursday morning between eight and eleven is fine."

"Great. Nine is fine with me. Please text me the address of where you want to meet, and I'll be there."

"Sounds like a plan to me. See you then. Have a great day."

I hung up the phone.

"Who was you talking to?"

Alonzo startled me, almost causing me to piss on myself.

"Oh, that was an old law school friend of mine. He's out here in the Atlanta area. I was surprised to find out his number was still the same after all these years. I'm trying to see if I could help him out 'round the office since I can't practice law anymore. We're meeting downtown on Thursday. I was hoping you could drop me off or something." That lie just rolled off my tongue so easily. There was no way I can give off any vibes. That shit ain't right.

"Shit, you know how to drive. You can take the truck. It has GPS so you can get around easily. I'll ride my bike. That way, you can spend as much time as you need without rushing back."

"Wow! I appreciate that. I need to go car shopping as soon as possible. I was thinking about a Lexus or Benz. Shoot, I need something fancy."

"I hear that, Ms. World Boss," he joked. "I just stopped by to pick up a package. I'm on my way back out."

"Oh, okay. I'm just here, trying to readjust to a little normalcy."

"A'ight, ma. I'll see you later."

Whew! That was close. I didn't hear when he came in. I had to be more careful—I couldn't afford to let anyone throw a monkey wrench in my plans. Not this time around. I'm older and a lot wiser now. I can't act on impulse or let my emotions get the best of me . . .

Azir Jackson

Our first night together was rough for me. From the minute I took the bitch to my crib, I was ready to blow her fucking head off. What was even worse, the bitch thought I was enjoying her pussy. Fuck nah! With every thrust I took deep inside of her, I was thinking about how I was going to kill her. Fucking her was only part of the plan to get her where the fuck I wanted her.

I really peeped the grimy side of this bitch when she started knockin' her gums 'bout my pops and my moms. It took everything in me not to smack the shit outta her. That smirk she had on her face when she talked about them irked my fucking nerves. This was my first time coming face-to-face with evil. Don't get me wrong; I'ma street nigga, so I see evil e'ery day, but this bitch was the devil herself. *Coldhearted bitch!* I thought.

My phone started ringing as I walked into the trap. I looked at the phone and saw it was my moms.

"Hello."

"Hey, baby. How you doing?"

"I'm good. Out here tryin'a handle a few things."

"Azir, you betta stay outta them streets. It's crazy. Did you see the news?"

"Nah, I 'ont watch TV. What, something happened?"

"Yea, Dwayne got gunned down in his driveway a few nights ago. I just got off the phone wit' his mother and sister. The police saying it was drug related, but his mother saying they think it's something else."

"Ma, I know you ain't crying over that nigga."

"Azir, regardless of what happened between me and him, they didn't have to kill him like that. He got a child, who is now fatherless. This senseless killing got to stop," she cried.

Man, I wasn't tryin'a hear all this. But it was my mom, and I knew she was feeling that bitch-ass nigga at one point. So I kept my opinion to myself to spare her feelings.

"Ma, this nigga was in these streets. He had a lot of enemies. It's hard to tell whose toes he done stepped on. It could be anybody, real talk."

"Hmm. As long as it ain't you, baby, 'cause Atlanta PD all over this one, and the feds are involved also. They said he was under federal indictment at the time."

"Nah, I ain't go near that nigga after the day I told you I saw him."

"That's good 'cause motherfuckas goin' start runnin' their mouth fo' that reward money. I wouldn't be surprised if your name gets thrown up in there. Shit, even mine, 'cause I used to date him. We just need to be prepared when they come snooping."

"Listen, Ma, I got to run; I be over there prob-ably tomorrow to see you and Nana."

Damn! Every time somebody got popped, I'm the first person Mom-dukes calls. Like really? I 'ont know why she would think that about me. Oh well, that nigga deserved e'erything he got for disrespecting me and mines.

I hung up the phone and walked into the room where my niggas were. It was time to handle business!

***

I dialed Natasha's number; I had to put her up on the game, which I knew was gonna cost me a couple of Gs. But it didn't matter because, without her, none of this would've been possible.

"Yo, let me in."

"Damn, boy, I just got in the bed," she complained jokingly.

"My bad. I was in the neighborhood."

"Uh-huh. Sure. I ain't heard from you in over a week."

"Shit, my bad. I've been busy. Business is booming, so I got to stay on top of it. Plus, I moved into my own crib. Shit, a nigga doing too much for real. I can't get a second to breathe."

"Well, more work mean mo' money. So wha' you complainin' fo'?" she laughed.

Shorty was cool as fuck, but not on my level. She was one of the females that you could chill with, smoke, drink, and talk shit with.

"So, listen, ole girl is out of prison."

"Who you talkin' 'bout?"

"Shayna."

"Boy, you lying. She got 'bout ten more years to do. 'Bout six with good time."

"Nah, her ass is out here. She's at my crib as we speak."

"What the fuck? What did I miss? Y'all messin' around?"

"Nah, it ain't like that. I can't get into the whys. Just trust me on this. She's been asking for you, say she wants to see you. You know she ain't no fool, so she might try to pick you 'bout if we really related or not."

"I ain't no fool. Her ass is only book smart. She 'ont have a lick of sense outside of that."

"Okay, I 'preciate it. Oh, I almost forgot . . . Here goes a li'l sump'n." I handed her five stacks.

"Oh my God. You're a savior. Boy, I freaking love youuuu!" She got up and walked over and hugged me.

"Damn, ma, it's only a few dollars. I know you could use it."

"And you just don't know how much I 'preciate you."

"A'ight, enough of this emotional shit. I'ma 'bout to bounce. I'll get at you."

"A'ight. One."

I left, jumped on my bike, and sped off. As I rode down the street, something ran through my mind. See, Natasha was cool and all, but she also could be bought if the price was right. With that said, she was a liability that I couldn't afford. Damn, I hated to think like this, but I ain't no fool, and besides, my freedom meant more to me than my loyalty to her!

Chapter Sixteen

Shayna Jackson

I got up, showered, and put on my pencil skirt and a collared shirt with a pair of Steve Madden heels. I looked myself over in the mirror. Shayna is back, bitches!

Then I grabbed my Michael Kors clutch and walked out of the condo. I put on my shades and opened his truck door. It was a nice ride, but I need a sexier car. Something that fit my style . . . fast and elegant.

We were meeting at the Marriott downtown. It was my idea to meet there; that way, I could be in control of the situation.

"Checking in, the name is Shayna Jackson."

"Good morning, ma'am. Here is your key to room 212. Enjoy your stay at the Marriott."

I took the key and headed for the elevator. I made sure I was forty-five minutes early. I ordered breakfast for my guest and me; then I lay in bed relaxing until I heard a knock on the door. I looked through the peephole and saw a stocky, old, bearded man standing on the other side.

"Yuck," I mumbled, but desperate times call for desperate measures . . .

"Hello, I'm Shayna." I extended my arm to him.

"Albert Richardson, but my friends call me Big Al."

"Come in. I ordered us some breakfast."

"Oh great. I ran out before I had a chance to eat."

We sat at the table and ate. I watched as he gulped down the food like a pig. Damn, Al was behaving like he ain't ate in ages. *Greedy fuck,* I thought.

After breakfast, he wiped his mouth, gulped some coffee, then spoke. "Miss Jackson, what can I do for you?"

"Well, Al, I'm looking for my long lost sister and her son. I haven't seen them since my nephew was a baby. That was some twenty-something years ago. Daddy recently passed away and left us a decent chunk of money. So here I am, trying to find the only family I have left. I hope you can help me."

"Well, I'll need some background info on her and the boy's age. My fee will—"

"Don't worry 'bout the fee. I'm far from broke, and this means everything to me." I rubbed his arm and looked at him seductively.

"Alrighty, then, let's get down to business. Start with names, possible date of birth, and last known address."

I didn't know too much 'bout the bitch, but I know her name and her last known address in Richmond. I gave him all the info that I remembered.

"Well, that's all I need. I'll get on this as soon as possible."

"Listen, Al, I need this information real soon. A day or two at the most." I took out a wad of cash and handed it to him to speed up the process.

"Oh wow, Miss Shayna, you know exactly how to make a man happy. The husband must be one lucky fella," he grinned.

"No, the husband was a fucking fool that didn't know what a gem he had. Are you married, Al? I don't see a ring."

"Yes, for twenty years now. The wife and I have three beautiful daughters."

"Tell me, Al, does your wife fuck you good?"

"Huh?" He looked puzzled.

"You heard me. Does yo' wife fuck you good?"

"Miss Sha, uh, Miss Shayna—"

"Don't bother to answer that," I cut him off. I walked over to him and knelt down in front of him. I started to unbutton his pants and took out his thick, short cock. There was nothing attractive about it, but it didn't matter. I got straight to the point. I took the little midget in my mouth and deep-throated it. It was short in length, but the width was a killer. Even though I was a pro, my damn mouth was tired.

"Aargh, aargh," his old ass groaned.

"Mmm-hmmm. I bet yo' wife can't suck you off this good," I teased, then went back to sucking him aggressively.

"Oh sweet Jesus, I'm 'bout to discharge," he yelled like a bitch.

I sucked harder while working his balls. I felt his cock getting harder. I let his dick go as sperm spurted out. There was no way I was goin' let his old juice flow down my damn throat.

He sat down on the bed, then leaned back and lay there grunting like a pig and holding his chest.

Lord, I hope this motherfucker is not having no heart attack, I thought.

"You all right, Albert?"

"Yes, yes. I'm so embarrassed. I've never experienced this feeling before. Oh, Lord."

"Albert, relax. You just haven't been wit' the right woman before."

"Yeah, my Doris is old-fashioned. She 'ont know how to do none of this stuff the younger generation be doing."

"Listen, Al, there's more of this where that came from. If you play your cards right, I might just let you get some of this good, high-grade pussy I got here." I patted my pussy.

"What you mean by playing my cards right?"

"Get me the info I need, keep this between us, and, I promise, you'll be havin' this feelin' for a long time." I got up and kissed him on the cheek.

"Okay, Albert, pull yo' pants up and get to work. I'm hoping to hear from you ASAP."

"Oh, Lord, my mind's so messed up; I'm just sittin' here exposing myself. Pardon me. Yes, I'm getting on it right away. I'll call you in a few days, pretty lady," he grinned at me.

Albert left, and I went to the bathroom and washed out my mouth with Listerine. See, I love fucking. All those years that I was in prison only made my sexual appetite stronger. I loved how powerful my pussy was and how men reacted to it. This time, I was scared that old fart was going to die on me. I can see the headlines now: MAN KILLED BY POWERFUL PUSSY. I chuckled to myself as I exited the hotel room.

I stopped by the front desk, handed over the key, put on my Prada glasses, and walked out of the lobby.

***

It's been weeks since I started fucking with Alonzo, and, as usual, I was tired and bored out of my damn mind while he was out running the streets. It reminds me of how Alijah was when I was married to him. It brought back memories of how much I hate being alone while he was out fucking other bitches. To clear my mind, I cut on the television to catch the news. Out of nowhere, an old friend came to my mind. The last I'd heard, he was retired. Soon as I get settled, I plan on visiting Sanderson. How could I forget about him? That son of a bitch double-crossed my ass. He will soon learn that *no one* crosses Shayna, and for that, he'd pay dearly.

The anxiety of finding Sierra and her bastard son was killing me. I could taste the sweetness of revenge on my tongue. This time, it won't be no "almost" killed her ass. On my daddy's life, I was going to finish her so she could join the bastard she so badly wanted. I was so ready to start the next chapter of my life, even considering a future with Alonzo. He did something to my heart; it was a feeling that I've never experienced before . . .

Weeks had passed, and I was nervous and getting restless. I needed to hear from Albert. He promised that I would hear from him in days.

I picked up the phone and dialed his number. He didn't pick up, so I called right back.

"Shayna, hey, you. I was gonna call you."

"Really? I thought you took my money, cheated me out of my head, and ran off."

"Ha-ha, no. I been in the business too long. Well, pretty lady, I think I found yo' sister and her son."

"You *think*, or you *did?* Spit it out."

"Yes, I found a Sierra Rogers; she's right here in Stone Mountain, Georgia."

The phone fell out of my hand . . . I snatched it up off the ground and put it back to my ear.

"Miss Jackson, are you there?"

"Yes, I'm here. The phone fell out of my hand. Sorry. I'm speechless. After all these years, you found my sister. Daddy would have been so happy that you found his baby girl. How sure are you that's my sister and not just some woman with the same name?"

"Umm, not a hundred percent sure as yet, but I'm pretty confident that I'm barking up the correct tree. I'm doing some deeper investigating. I had to smile when I found out she was here. Y'all might be living next to each other and don't even know it," he chuckled.

"I got to go; let me know what else you find out," I said, then hung up in his face.

"Jerk." I don't see what the point was of him telling me this if he wasn't 100 percent sure that it was her.

Sierra in Georgia, I thought. If it turned out to be her, I wondered how long ago she moved here. I would never forget that bitch's face. The entire time I was locked up, I'd dreamed about meeting up with her again. I wanted it to be phenomenal. This time around would be our last encounter. No more loose ends this time or me going to prison. I also planned on getting that bitch mother. I've never forgotten how she got on that stand and pleaded with the judge to give me life. That bitch painted a horrible picture of me. She had it out for me ever since I met her ass. She should've minded her own business because now, she was going to be one dead bitch too.

I poured me a glass of Moscato and walked upstairs. I'm happy I was home alone this time, so I could get some time to put my thoughts together. Plus, laying up with me and not making money was a no-no.

I walked into the room and placed my drink on the nightstand; then I walked over to the dresser to get me a pair of my pajama pants. Suddenly, I stopped dead in my tracks. The drawer was half-closed. I hurriedly pulled it open and noticed that my clothes were not the way I left them. I stuck my hand under the clothes and pulled out my envelope . . . Anger erupted in my heart as I noticed that the envelope had been pried open. I ripped it open and saw all my papers all over the place and not in order like I had them. I knew somebody's nosy ass went through my shit, because I was a neat freak, and I'd placed each piece of paper neatly into the envelope before I sealed it up. I never opened it; I didn't have any reason to.

What would possess this nigga to go through my shit? He straight violated me. What was he looking for? Who is he?

"Sierra and her son are living in the Atlanta area," Albert's voice played back in my mind!

"No. Ain't no way. He can't be Sierra's son. That boy can't be nothing but a little over twenty-something. Hell no!" I tried to convince myself. I needed to find out what was going on, but how? I already went through his belongings, searched the house from top to bottom and found no evidence of anything discriminating. Quickly, I gulped my drink as I racked my brain for answers.

After a few moments, it came to me. The one person that was related to him—she should be able to set my mind at rest. I dialed Natasha's number.

After a few rings, she picked up.

"Hello, who this?" she answered with an attitude.

"Girl, this Shayna, your old bunkie."

"Oh shoot, Shayna, what the heck you doing out, girl?"

"Long story. I'll tell you one of these days, but I'm here in ATL."

"You lying. What you doing in the A, girl? I thought you were from New York."

"Yo' cousin convinced me to come out here, and that's correct. I was born and raised in New York."

"Girl, stop playing. I knew he was crazy, but I had no idea you were too. I see he's really into you if he got you out here wit' him."

"Really . . . Natasha, tell me how come he has a Jamaican accent, and you don't? I thought y'all grew up together."

"Yeah, well, umm, he grew up 'round his father's side of the family."

"Hmm, really? Why don't I believe you? I've spent years with you; we talked about everything and not once did you mention a cousin named Alonzo. What's wrong with this picture?"

"Shayna, are you accusing me of something? If so, come out and say it. All this beating around the bush, I ain't got time for it," she replied angrily.

"No, I'm not accusing you of anything, at least not yet. But I know you is a fucking liar. I know y'all ain't no cousins. What I don't know is, who is he and why y'all lying."

"Listen, bitch, unless you got proof that he ain't my motherfucking cousin, don't call my phone accusing me of shit. I've never disrespected you in any way. Maybe you are too used to fucked-up-ass niggas that you can't accept a real nigga. I'm done talkin' to yo' ass," she said.

The dial tone rang out in my ear. I chuckled to myself. *That bitch is a poor liar. I can see a lying bitch from a mile away,* I thought.

Alonzo or whatever your name is, what is your business with me? What the fuck had I gotten myself into? Wait, I must be trippin'; I been here with this nigga. If he wanted to kill me, he could have by now. Maybe I'm paranoid . . . or am I just ignoring the signs?

I showered and dressed. I needed to get me a gun. I knew I couldn't walk up in no store and get one. I needed to come up with a plan first . . .

After sucking and sliding this pussy over on Albert's cock, he agreed to get me a gun. It took a little convincing. I had no problem showin' him the bruise on my arm from my boyfriend roughing me up. He was just another lame-ass nigga trying to rescue a damsel in distress.

Albert got me a 9mm semiautomatic pistol. He handed it to me after we left the gun store.

I took it out of the box and admired it. I hadn't held a gun in years, and just the sight sent electric shocks throughout my body.

"Be careful wit' that, pretty lady. Guns are nothing to be played wit' and only use it if your life is in danger."

"I understand. I wouldn't hurt a fly. I only need this to scare him off when he tries to beat me," I burst out crying.

"I don't know this fella, but he has no business hitting on a lady like you. I have some friends in DeKalb County Police Headquarters that I can call up for a favor if you want. He better watch out."

"Oh, thank you, but I don't think it'll go that far."

"Okay, pretty lady. I gotta go meet up wit' this client."

He drove me back to where the truck was parked.

"Thank you again, Albert." I winked at him, got out of his car, and walked over to the truck.

Quickly, I wiped my tears and got into the truck. I marveled at the sight of my new toy. Oh, I felt like the old me again. For a minute, I'd felt vulnerable because I had no protection. This was all I needed so niggas or bitches could know . . . I was not a bitch to be played with!

Chapter Seventeen

Sierra Rogers

For days, Azir lay heavily on my mind; each time that I cut on the television, there seemed to be more news about Dwayne's death. I continued to pray to God; I needed him to protect my only child. I was considering asking him to leave Atlanta, maybe visit England where his father's side of the family was or go back to Jamaica. Atlanta wasn't the place for him, and the last thing I needed was for him to be wrapped up in some bullshit he had nothing to do with. I needed to talk with him but not over the phone. I needed to see him.

I jumped up and grabbed my purse. Azir had written down his address the last time he came over. I fumbled around until I found the piece of paper.

5202 Abbey Street, Conyers, Georgia

I grabbed my keys, ran down the stairs, and jumped into my car.

I cut the music on high so I could tune out some of the thoughts that were running through my mind, put his address in the GPS, and headed to his condo.

I tried calling him so I could tell him I was on my way to see him, but his phone went straight to voice mail. I sent out a text to him. Twenty-five minutes later, I pulled up at the address. These were some nice condos, and they looked brand new, I thought. I kept calling him but still didn't get any answer, which was strange. I've never called him when he never answered or texted me back. My stomach started to get queasy.

"God, where is my son?" I asked.

I got out and went to ring his bell numerous times, but still no answer. I stood outside for a few minutes, then walked back to my car. I sat in the car and kept redialing his number, but there was still no answer.

I was getting worried; I wished he'd pick up his phone or text me so I would know he was all right. I held my head up and looked around. Out of the corner of my eye, I glimpsed the figure of a woman. I swore that she looked like . . . I laughed to myself. *Sierra, you trippin'*, I thought. I watched as she walked over to Azir's door; I wanted to jump out to make sure she was going to ring the correct doorbell. Only to my astonishment, she didn't ring the doorbell. She pushed a key in, opened the door, and shut it behind her.

"Who the fuck was that entering my son's home?" I asked myself. I decided to sit tight, even though everything in me was yelling to go see who that was. I anxiously sat in my car with my seat laid back. Ten minutes later, this same woman exited the home and walked toward my car. "*What the fuck?*" I yelled. Shayna . . . No! What the hell was Shayna, the bitch that tried to kill me, doing at my son's house? I watched as she jumped in Azir's truck. I wanted to jump out of my car and approach her, but common sense told me not to. I needed to find out what was going on here. Again, I looked down at the piece of paper where Azir wrote his address.

5202 Abbey Street, Conyers, Georgia

None of this made sense. All I knew was that something was not fucking right. I thought that bitch was in the feds and wasn't supposed to be released for another ten years.

Maybe Azir made a mistake when he wrote the address down; but no, I knew his truck, and the license plate matched his. I knew this for sure because he's on my insurance. I watched as she drove out of the subdivision.

There were still no calls or texts from Azir. There was no need to hang around. I drove like a madwoman all the way back to Stone Mountain. I sped into my driveway, parked, and jumped out. I hurriedly opened the door and ran into the house.

"You all right? What's wrong?" Jeanette asked.

"I need to check something online real quick." I jumped on the Internet and typed in Bureau of Prisons' inmate locator. I typed in Shayna Jackson and her federal identification number, which I got from my lawyer years ago.

Inmate released.

I blinked twice and read it again. Nothing changed. It said "Inmate released" right in front of my eyes. I felt tears well up in my eyes, and my chest tightened. Quickly, I grabbed my cell and called my lawyer back in Richmond. He wasn't in, so I asked his secretary if she knew anything about Shayna Jackson's early release from prison. She told me the office was informed that she was released early, based off an incident that happened at the prison. She also told me that the news was so big, weeks ago, it was all over CNN. I thanked her and hung up the phone. So these motherfuckers knew this bitch was released and nobody bothered to let the victim know? This fucking justice system was a damn joke.

"Man, *nooo! Nooo!*" I screamed out and threw the computer into the wall, leaving a big hole there and breaking the screen.

Jeanette rushed into the den and looked at me, then looked at the hole I put in the wall.

"Sierra, what's going on? Talk to me. Did something happen to Azir?" She looked at me frantically.

"What's going on is that bitch Shayna is out of prison and is here in Georgia—at my son's house!"

"What? Sierra, are you sure? You seen her with your own two eyes? Maybe you just paranoid, baby. That bitch put you through so much."

I stood up and walked over to the window and stared outside, looking at nothing in particular.

"I was missing Azir something serious. I called his phone, but he didn't answer. When I got there, he wasn't home. So I sat in the car waiting, and I saw a woman with the same facial features as Shayna. She opened Azir's door. I still wasn't sure it was her. I sat and waited; then she came back out, and that's when I saw her face clearly, and to prove I'm not trippin', she jumped in Azir's truck. I know his truck and his license plate. Jeanette, I'm telling you, this sick bitch is here in Georgia and around my child."

"Have you heard from Azir?"

"No. I've been calling him nonstop, but he's not answering my calls or my texts; so unlike him. Jeanette, this bitch shot me twice. I will *not* sit around and wait for her to hurt me, my son, or you. I checked the fed's Web site, and it said 'released.' I am *not* trippin'."

"That judicial system does not protect the victim. This woman should've never been able to walk these streets again, let alone be in the same state as you and Azir. Why hasn't anyone notified you about this?"

There was no need to sit around talking 'bout the system. I went upstairs and grabbed my gun; also took out an extra clip. This ho lucked up twice; there was no way she was going to creep up on me a third time without me killing that deranged bitch.

I walked back downstairs; my mind was speeding, and my thoughts were nothing nice. This bitch had to die. I can't allow her ever to do anything else to me and my family. I had an instant flashback of when that bitch shot me the second time. I remember hearing Jeanette screaming and praying. That memory brought tears. I felt fucked up and angry all over again. I tried hard to control the tears that were forming. Not because I was scared of this bitch, but because my soul was filled with anger and hate.

"Sierra, I don't know how I feel about this woman here. I hate her for all the pain she's put you through. I dreamed of killing her many nights after she shot you. I had to beg God to take the hate outta my heart, 'cause I hated her. And for you to tell me that she's around Azir is hurting me. I . . . I . . . I can't even think right now. Jesus, take the wheel."

I didn't say a word, because I was speechless. I looked at Jeanette, shook my head, and headed out the door. This time, I was more vigilant of my surroundings. I got on I-285. I was heading to Clayton County toward the gun store.

"Hello, miss. How may I help you?"

"I want two guns. Powerful enough to blow somebody's head off." I looked at him.

He looked at me kind of weird; I guess he didn't like how it sounded.

"No, nothing like that. I'm a businesswoman, and I need protection, especially with all the latest killings going on 'round here."

"I understand, and you have the right to bear arms."

He showed me a variety of guns that could do some bodily harm: the .380, 9 mm, .40 S&W, and the .45 ACP.

"Hmm, I already have a .380, so let me see the 9 mm and .45 ACP." I decided to get them both. I was going to be prepared this time around. I gave him my ID and paid for my guns. I wasn't no killer, nor did I want to be one, but what I will not have is this bitch interrupting my life and playing with my child's life.

I got in the car and saw that I had a missed call from Azir. I took a deep breath and pressed the call button.

"Yo, ma, you a'ight? I got 'bout twenty calls from you and Grandma."

"Yes, I was checking up on you. I stopped by the house, but you wasn't home."

"You stopped by the house? I was out in Marietta handlin' some business. What, sump'n happened?"

"No, I was just missing my baby. You know ever since you moved out, I don't see you that much."

"Oh, okay. I'm back on this side of town. We can meet up for lunch."

"Great, meet me at the house."

"Bet." He hung up the phone.

Sigh . . . So my son is still alive. I started to call back to find out what was going on but decided against it at the last minute. I wasn't any fool, but I planned on finding out everything one way or another.

***

I heard the door open, and I knew it was Azir. I got up and walked toward the door.

"Hey, baby, I'm ready. You're driving your truck or want me to drive my car?"

"I'm on the bike, so you can drive."

"The bike? What's wrong wit' yo' car?"

"Nothing; it's parked at the crib."

"Oh, okay. I was over your house, and I thought I seen a woman in your truck." I looked at him to see how he would react.

"Hell nah. I'm the only one that drives my truck. Maybe somebody over there have one similar to mine," he blatantly lied to my face. I know my child, and I also know his truck.

"Yeah, I know you wouldn't let anyone else drive the truck, especially since the insurance is in my name," I said as I pulled off.

"I was thinking about Red Lobster unless you have something else in mind."

"Nah, Red Lobster good."

On the ride to Red Lobster, we chatted about general things. I sensed he was kind of distant, but I continued talking to him. The key was to keep the dialogue between us open.

We ordered our food and sat waiting. The waitress brought us those good-ass biscuits before our meals were served, but I wasn't hungry.

"So, baby, how is it going over at the house?"

"Everything cool. I'm enjoying the freedom. Now I can have all the company I want over," he laughed.

"Yeah, 'cause you know that was not happenin' in my house," I laughed, but I was dead-ass serious.

"I know; plus, I'm grown, so it's only right that I get my own anyway."

"Yeah, ain't nothin' like yo' own. Azir, I saw the news about Dwayne's death, and they have an eyewitness that told the police that they saw a bike speed away from the scene of the shooting."

He looked at me, then said, "I 'ont understand why you telling me this. I told you the other day I ain't got nuttin' to do with it."

"I know, baby. It's just that I want to make sure you tellin' me the truth." I stared into his eyes.

He took my hands and held them tight. "Ma, I promise you, I ain't had nothing to do wit' that man gettin' shot. I mean, this nigga had enemies all over the A. Any one of them could've killed him."

Tears rolled down my face. Call it a mother's intuition, or maybe it was because I looked into his eyes, but I could tell he was hiding something from me.

Our food came; I barely touched mine. I tried my best not to let on because I didn't want to alert him that something was wrong.

"Azir, your grandma and I wanted to come by Sunday if you don't mind."

"Nah, y'all welcome to come by anytime, but I might be out of town the weekend. We can do it once I get back in town."

"Azir, what? You have a woman over there that you don't want us to see?"

"Nah, I'm the only one there. I ain't got time for no female. You know how needy y'all get." He busted out laughing.

"Boy, 'y'all'? I ain't never been needy. Not yo' mama. Baby, I know you heard all the stories about Shayna, your daddy's wife."

"Yeah, what about her? She shot you twice and set Dad up. That's all y'all was willin' to tell me."

"Well, I found out yesterday that she's released from prison. This woman is obsessed wit' me, so I have no idea where she's going, or what she has in mind. I need you to be extra careful of your surroundings."

"Damn, Ma, you acting all spooky and shit. Shayna or whatever her name is ain't that crazy to come 'round while I'm alive. Ma, I will protect you at any cost. Believe that. She betta keep her crazy ass outta Georgia," he said angrily.

I looked at Azir; I could see that he was genuinely upset, but I still couldn't shake the feeling he was keeping something from me. I knew that she was in his home and driving his truck, and he failed to mention it, even when I asked. Azir was hiding something. I just hoped he knew what he was doing, 'cause that bitch was deadly as a rotten snake!

We got back to the house, and as Azir started to leave, he turned back to me and said, "Ma, I love you wit' e'erything in me. I will protect you by any means necessary." He then walked off, jumped on his bike, and sped off.

I stood outside for a minute; then I turned around and walked into the house. Jeanette was sitting in the living room.

"So what did Azir say?"

"Nothing. He say he ain't do anything to dude."

"You believe him?"

"Yes, he's my son. So his word is good enough for me. Plus, Dwayne had enemies all over ATL."

"Hmmm . . ."

"You think he did it, don't you? You already found him guilty!" I shouted.

Her ass was pissing me off with her judgmental self. I done told her ass he didn't do it, but she sat up there behaving like he was guilty.

"Sierra, I never said he did anything. Stop putting words in my mouth."

"You ain't had to say it; your actions speak for itself. I ain't goin' argue wit' you, Jeanette. I got a bigger problem on my hands; Azir is hiding something. He never mentioned anyone staying wit' him. I don't know what's going on, but I do know Shayna is there at my son's house."

"I'm still in shock; I thought about calling the police and sending them over there, 'cause I believe that trick is up to no good. I still can't figure out what she and Azir have going on, and if she knows that's your son. Is she using him to get to you? And do he even know who she is? All I can do is pray to God. He has to protect my grandbaby."

Jeanette immediately bowed her head and prayed, "Lord, have mercy on my grandbaby soul and deliver him from that evil witch."

"Well, I'm not goin' sit around and let that bitch hurt my child. See, I have the upper hand; she has no idea that I saw her, and Azir has no idea because I didn't tell him."

"Sierra, please be careful. We should call the police and let them know what's going on."

"Fuck the police. Did you forget that they were the ones that brought that bitch in my home in the first place? Then they turned around and killed Alijah. I don't fuckin' respect them. This bitch tried to kill me and still managed to be out here. I got this; I was never a punk, and I will let this bitch know that her luck done ran out!"

Azir Jackson

Now wasn't the time anyway, especially 'cause Shayna was at the crib. The last thing I needed was for Mom-dukes and her to bump heads. I already knew if they did, someone was going to get hurt, and I would miss out on murking that bitch myself.

I wish my moms would stop pressing me so much. I hate lying to her, but the shit she asking about, ain't no way I could tell her the truth. The less she knew, the better it was for her. She's my mother and all, but I didn't trust anyone but myself, because I knew I would never confess.

It was almost time for me to get up out of Atlanta. Business was straight, but my heart's tellin' me it was time to move around. I thought 'bout moving to New York or Miami. I knew I would leave my crew behind, but I needed to stay out of the way. Live a little and spend some of this money. I live for these streets, but my heart was into making my music. I made enough money where I could fund my own studio and all the equipment that I might need. Yeah, I was about to put some of this illegal money to good use.

Shayna's behavior was kind of off lately. I pretended like I didn't notice, but I did. Ever since this bitch been at the house, I haven't gotten any sleep. There was no way I was going to let my guard down around her ass. Instead, each night she lay up in my arms, and I'd closed my eyes, pretending like I was asleep. In reality, I was lying there plotting my next move!

Speaking of her ass, I wonder where she's at. She left hastily this morning. I was sitting in the cut on my bike when she pulled off in my truck. At first, I was gonna follow her but changed my mind. Instead, I decided to go back in the house. I locked the door behind me and went upstairs. It was to see what was going on with this ho. "Gotcha," I mumbled, as I decided to search the drawer where she kept her things. I rambled through her underwear until my hand bumped into an envelope that hidden underneath the neatly folded clothes.

"Well well well. Let's see what you got here," I said as I sat on the edge of the bed. I was careful not to rip the envelope . . . My grandma had paperwork on shit that went down, and my mother told me the story of how things went down with my dad and this bitch. However, seeing that this bitch kept files on the grimy shit she did to my family ignited the fumes. The bitch had clippings of my mom's shooting, newspaper clippings on my daddy, and a statement that she made to the law. Everything was right in front of me in black and white. I knew then I couldn't stand to be around this bitch any longer. I had to put my plan into motion tonight, not a minute later.

I continued going through the papers when my phone vibrated on my side and interrupted my thoughts.

"Yo, wha a gwaan, brethren?"

"Wey yuh deh?"

"Mi deh a di yaad, no deh pon nuttin'."

"Man, the police boy den hit di spot."

"Wha the fuck yuh a tell mi?" I yelled in the phone.

"Yo, Trevor just hit me and sey dat."

"Yo, meet me pon Panola in twenty minutes, right at the Quick Trip."

"Bet, Boss man."

"Yo, fuck!" I hit the dresser with my fist.

I pushed the paper back in the envelope and stuck it back in the drawer, then quickly shut it.

I ran downstairs, locked the door, and jumped on my bike. As I raced through the subdivision, my heart was pounding fast. If this was true and

Babylon went up in the trap, that would mean they got work and money. What the rassclaat, I thought. How the fuck? Nah, fuck that. *Who* the fuck been running their mouth was the question that I needed to be answered.

I pulled over to the gas station where my man was waiting in his F-150 truck, pulled up beside him, and jumped off the bike.

"Yo, what the pussyclaat a gwaan?"

"Yo, just got another call from Jerry. They got him and Mike down at DeKalb County."

"Damn! You ain't said that they got these niggas."

"Mi never know until a few minutes ago. Yeah, $50,000 bond apiece."

"Yo, call the lawyer bwoy pon Ponce De Leon and get him to bond dem out. And, yo, bless them with some paper, hit the lawyer off, and cut all ties wit' them niggas. Sump'n ain't pussyclaat right. We got a rat up in the camp, yo. Mi nuh trust none a dem bwoy ya."

"Is the same ting I was tinkin'. Shit hot right now, but outta nowhere. I mean, in order fi di police dem know the stash house, a nigga got to tell them. The question is, who is the rat?"

"Yo, mi know a nuh me and a nuh yuh. Other don dat, mi nuh trust these pussyhole niggas," I yelled.

I was mad as fuck—just when I was tryin'a bounce out of the place. I had a whole shipment of work and money that had just come. Now, all that shit was gone.

"Yo, all the fucking money. This shit hurt, yo."

"Trust mi; I feel the same friggin' way."

"So what's the move?"

"We need to lie low for a minute. Yo, I might be bouncing in a few, tryin'a go up top to pursue this music shit."

"Word, my nigga. Dat's what I'm talkin' 'bout."

"Yeah, so I'ma need you to run things fi mi."

"Brethren, yuh done know sey I got you."

"Yeah, yo, just don't trust none a those Yankee niggas. The pussyhole dem don't really like we. If the Babylon run up in a di spot, then trust mi, dem know sump'n, you feel me?"

"Yeah, mon. I'ma get a whole new team."

"A'ight, yo, I'ma hit you tomorrow. In the meantime, find a new stop. Some work coming in Wednesday. This between you and me. From this point on, can't trust these niggas."

"A'ight, Boss man."

I revved my bike up, and sped through the Quick Trip parking lot, then rode out into traffic. In the corner of my eyes, I peeped a black Yukon Denali wit' tinted glass pull out and get into traffic behind me. I decided to pull into the next plaza, where I watched as the Denali drove past. I couldn't see inside, but I smelled feds from a distance away. Then I pulled back out and into traffic.

Chapter Eighteen

Sierra Rogers

I stopped by the shop to let my workers know that I wasn't going to be in. I had important "family matters" to handle. I prepared myself mentally for what was about to pop off.

This bitch was back in the picture, driving my son's truck like nothing. Ever since Azir lied to me, I knew sump'n was up. Part of me wanted to storm up in his condo and blow this bitch head off. Instead, I followed this bitch 'round town for days. Every time she left the house, I would pull out behind her. I even saw when she met up wit' some old dude, and they went into the gun store. She ran around like she had no worries. This bitch had no idea that I was on to her. I knew for a fact that she lived with Azir. Every night when she went in, I stayed in my car until Azir made it home.

In a matter of days, I could tell this bitch's entire schedule and meals. I haven't showered in days and barely ate anything. I couldn't afford to leave, because I needed to know where this bitch was at, at all times. Nights were extra hard, because Azir was up in the house with her. He was still lying to me like he had no company or he wasn't home. I had no idea why my child was doing what he was doing; all I knew was his life was in danger. None of this made sense to me. How the fuck did Azir even meet this bitch as much I prayed to God to keep this bitch away? I had no idea why he would allow this wickedness back into our lives. I was confused.

Each night, I begged God to protect my only seed. Only tonight was different. I know she has a gun, and her intentions for my son were not good. I had to think of something fast.

I went home to get some things in order and have a talk with Jeanette. I knew if there was anyone that I could depend on, it would be her. No matter what, I knew Azir and I were her heart, and she would be there if we ever needed her. Well, this was it.

We needed her.

I got my three guns and extra clips. I put one in my jacket pocket, one in my purse, and the other under the seat in my car. I put the extra clip in my glove compartment. I had on my black sweatpants, a black thermal, and a black hat along with my black Jordans. Jeanette got in the car, and I pulled off.

"You ready? Remember everything we talked about."

"I'm ready as can be. Sierra, please be careful. Remember, this bitch is a loose cannon and has nothing to lose. You, on the other hand, have *everything* to lose," she warned.

"Jeanette, I got this." I left it at that.

I didn't know what I was getting myself into, but what I did know was my son was in danger, and I had no choice but to get to him. This ho had no business coming to Atlanta, and for that, her ass would pay!

My emotions were running high. I was feeling anxious, and my adrenaline was rushing. My palms were sweaty, and my chest tightened as I approached the condo.

I breathed slowly to control my anger. I couldn't risk getting an anxiety attack at a time like this. I slowly coached myself back down to a normal pace.

Azir Jackson

I decided to head home after that hit we took earlier. I needed to get fucked up. I had a bad vibe 'bout everything that went down. Dude said the warrant said an informant told them 'bout the spot. That right there bothered me, 'cause it meant a rat was runnin' around. I didn't take that lightly. Back home in Jamaica when a nigga snitch, you straight cut his motherfuckin' head off, and if you can't find him, you kill his entire family. Not in America; these rat-ass niggas got mad love on the streets.

I noticed Shayna was already in the house. I was tired of being around this snake bitch too. The only reason why I ain't body her yet is because the timing wasn't right. I also love the fact that I was mentally torturing this bitch. Each time I'm with her, I envision all the shit I want to do to her—not sexually. Sometimes, I want to shoot her; sometimes, I want to use a machete and chop her up into tiny pieces. No matter how gruesome the scenes are that I have playing out in my head, it never seems to satisfy my taste for revenge. I was pressed for time now, and I know that I would have to deal with this bitch sooner than later.

"Hey, babes," she greeted me as I entered the house.

"What's good, love?" I barely mumbled.

"I picked us up some Chinese food. I was too tired to cook."

"That's cool. I ain't hungry anyway."

I headed to the bar and poured me a shot of Hennessy. I hope this bitch didn't say or do the wrong thing, 'cause the way I was feeling, I could just rip her head off with my bare hands. That's the kind of mood I was in.

After I got my drink, I went upstairs in the bedroom so I could roll me a blunt.

A few minutes later, Shayna joined me. Her eyes looked glassy, like she'd been drinking.

"You a'ight?"

"Yeah, I'm fine. Think I had a little too much to drink."

"Oh, okay. You got to take it easy on the bottle. You ain't no pro," I laughed.

Suddenly, we both heard the doorbell ring.

"Who the heck is that? Are you expecting someone?" Shayna quizzed.

"Nah, but it might be my homeboy. He supposed to drop a package off for me."

I got up out of bed and walked out of the room. I hope it wasn't my moms; this wasn't the time to get a visit. I looked through the peephole and saw it was my grandma outside, barefoot. I opened the door and stepped out. I couldn't even speak; I was shocked at the sight of my nana.

"Nana, what the heck you doing here?" I managed to utter.

"Azir, baby, I didn't know where else to go or who to turn to. Come over here. I don't want anyone to hear me, please."

I stepped away from the door and walked toward the curb. I was scared Shayna might overhear our conversation.

"Nana, I'm not understanding. What's going on? Have you been drinking? I smell alcohol on your breath."

"Azir, baby, I try not to touch anything, but I couldn't resist. Baby, give me a little piece of rock, I need a fix real bad." She grabbed my arms.

"Nana, stop it. I ain't giving you nothing. You've been clean for a minute. What happened to you? Did somebody get you hooked again? Nana, I can't help you. I know how bad my moms gonna be hurt if she finds out you've been using again."

"Azir, baby, please don't tell her. She'll kick me out. You can't," she pleaded.

"Nana, ain't that her car? Do she know you got it?"

"Yes, I asked her if I could go to the store."

"Damn, yo, you need to get back to the house, and you need to get back in NA. Nana, you come too far to turn back now. Go on home, Nana. I'll be over there to check on you. I love you."

"Azir, just a li'l piece. Please, I won't say a word," she pleaded as I walked her to where the car was parked.

She cried loudly as she pulled off, still begging me to give her a piece of rock. Man, my day just couldn't get any worse. I couldn't believe that this was my nana behaving like that. I heard the stories of her getting high back in the day, but I'd never witnessed it until now . . .

I was zoned out from the shit that happened. I turned around and walked toward the door. That's when I realized that I left the door open. I could only hope that bitch didn't hear anything that we said. The last thing I needed was her figuring things out.

I locked the door behind me and walked upstairs. She was lying in bed, watching TV.

"Is everything okay wit' you?"

"Yes, that was my homeboy's mom. She stopped by to pick up some money I owed him."

"All right. I was worried when you didn't come back in. You know I just got out of jail, so my nerves are bad," she laughed.

There was something 'bout that laugh that caught my attention. I knew something was up for sure when she winked at me. This bitch was up to no good, I thought as I sat on the bed.

Chapter Nineteen

Shayna Jackson

I was trying to figure out what was going on with Alonzo. His mood was different when he came home; I wonder if it was because of what he found in the drawer and what business it was to him. Maybe he was Alijah's son, and he was on to me, or was it that I was on to his bullshit . . .

I played it cool when he came home. In fact, I ordered us Chinese food, only to find out he wasn't hungry. I didn't let that spoil my mood; I remained calm, cool, and collected. What fucked up my mood was when the doorbell rang. I saw the strange look on his face; I would've given anything to be able to read his mind. I tried to tiptoe to the stairs to hear what he was saying, but I couldn't hear, so I went back to the bedroom. My nosy ass couldn't sit still, so I walked over to the window; I stood to the side, careful not to be seen. I saw him talking to an older woman. After a few minutes, she got into a car and pulled off. I ran back to bed, pretending like I was watching television the entire time. But first, I placed my gun underneath the pillow and lay on top of it.

He came back into the room, looking slightly irritated. I took a long look at him, and for the first time, I saw the resemblance of Alijah. I sat there frozen in disbelief. It was like I was looking at the spittin' image of that dead bastard. *How did I miss that?* I thought.

I sat up in the bed; my mind was racing. Everything around me seemed out of place. I felt delusional. It wasn't any coincidence when he contacted me. Did he know who I was all along? How did he know to find Natasha and get her to go along with his lies?

"Let me ask you something. Is your dad alive?"

"Nah, he passed away awhile back," he answered.

"That must be hard on you; you know boys are usually close with their fathers."

"Yeah, it was, but I'm maintaining."

"If you don't mind me asking, how did he die?"

"Some accident. Not really sure." He looked at me, those cold eyes and nose flared up, the same way Alijah would've done when he was irritated.

"How old are you? You are 'bout twenty-something?"

"I never told you my age. How would you know that?"

"I know—because I was your nanny when you were a baby." I pulled my gun from under the pillow and pointed it at him.

"Is that right, love?" He chuckled and pointed his gun at me.

"See, I'm not no fool. I knew there was something 'bout you, but until I spoke to Natasha and caught her in a lie, that's when I knew for sure you was an imposter."

"Yo, you trippin'. I don't know who you think I am, but I'm not that nigga. Put down your gun before you hurt yo'self. See, I put mine down. I'm fuckin' in love with you, woman." He looked me dead in the eyes.

"You don't fuckin' love me. You look just like my husband. I know you're here because of him," I yelled.

"Shayna, listen up, babe; I saw your pic, and I liked it. I came after you, 'cause you're the kind of woman that I need. I don't know anything 'bout none of this shit you talkin' 'bout or being some nigga's son that I don't even know. My pop's name ain't no damn Alijah."

"You're a fuckin' liar. I don't fuckin' believe you," I screamed and waved the gun at him.

"Be careful how you moving that pistol around. Yo, it don't make no sense. You been around here for weeks. If I wanted to kill you, I could've. I'm a real nigga, and I do real nigga shit. I need you in my life, shorty. Believe that."

Hmm . . . He did make a valid point. I've been here for a while sleeping in the same bed. He could've killed me, but he didn't. *Oh Lord, what have I done? Did I fuck up with the only man that cares about me?* I thought. My mind was telling me one thing, but my heart was screaming at me. I was confused and didn't know what to do. I lowered my gun and started to cry.

"Come here, shorty." He took the gun out of my hand.

I walked over to him and sat beside him. He put his arm around me, then spoke. "You know what one of the rules in the street is?" he asked.

"No, what is it?" I managed to say.

"Always follow your gut instinct, bitch."

I felt a gun pressed against my neck. I tried to reach for my gun, but he had a grip on my neck.

"You fuckin' liar. I trusted you!" I yelled.

"My pops trusted you too. Yes, my name is Azir Jackson. The only seed of the man you set up."

"Fuck you! Fuck you! How did I not see you for the piece of shit you are?" I hollered. Fuck crying—I was steaming with anger. I got tricked by this young-ass nigga. *Shayna, you done fucked up,* a voice in my head whispered.

He pushed me away from him and on the ground. Then he got up and stood over me.

"Bitch, get on the floor. See, ever since I was a little boy, I dreamt of this day. The day that I would look you in the eyes and watch you beg for yo' life—right before I blow your fucking head off."

He took a step closer and aimed the gun at my head. I knew then I didn't have a chance. *I should've killed the little monkey years ago when I had the chance,* I thought bitterly.

Chapter Twenty

Sierra Rogers

"Don't do that, son. Step away from that bitch. She's all mine," I said, as I entered the room with my 9 mm pointed at that wicked ho.

"Ma, what are you doin' here? And how did you get in here?" Azir looked at me with a shocked expression written all over his face.

"Not now, Azir. Well, hello, Mrs. Shayna Jackson. I see we meet once again," I said with conviction in my voice while I pointed the gun at that ho, not flinching even once.

"Wow! A family reunion, I see. Hello, Sierra, I should've killed yo' ass those two times I had the chance," she said and tried to spit on me.

I moved slowly toward this ho and knelt down beside her, right where Azir had his foot holding her down.

"I agree; you should've killed me. But guess what? You was a coward-ass bitch that fucked up—twice. Ha-ha. Don't you wish you paid attention to your instructor at the shooting range? No, ho, *you're* the stupid bitch. See, yo' dumb ass tried to kill me twice over a fuckin' dick. Bitch, it wasn't that fucking serious. There are a million and one dicks in this world, but, nah, yo' ass couldn't deal wit' the fact that he did not want that old, stretched-out, no-walls-havin' pussy. You were mad that he wanted this young pussy." I fired a shot into her left leg.

"Do something! This crazy bitch trying to kill me!" she yelled to Azir.

"Ma, I got this!" Azir said.

"Get out of my way—now, Azir! This bitch made my life hell for years. As a matter of fact, get the fuck out of the room. Get out!" I yelled.

"I ain't leaving you, Ma. Mi 'bout to shoot dis bitch in the head."

"No! That's way too easy. Now go!"

"Now, you, stand up and take yo' fucking clothes off," I demanded.

"Fuck you; I'm not takin' shit off. Kill me if you're going to, bitch. You won't get away wit' this. I'm well-connected, and it's only a matter of time before the feds is all over this."

This psychotic bitch leaped toward me and knocked the gun out of my hand. I hit that ho in the throat, but that didn't faze her; instead, she tried to go for the gun on the ground. I ran up to that ho and started punching her in the face. I didn't stop until blood started gushing from her eyes.

She grabbed my weave and scratched my face, but her strength was nothing compared to my rage. I was out to kill this ho. I used my boots and kicked that fragile ho into the nightstand, knocking her to the ground.

"Now, let's try this again, ho. Take off yo' fuckin' clothes." I pressed the gun against her temple.

"I'm not taking shit off. Go ahead and shoot me, bitch. You will still be a dirty-ass, project ho. Fuck you *and* that bastard of yours," she spat.

I fired a shot into her right knee.

"Aargh, you stupid bitch! You shot me again," she screamed.

"Bitch, take off yo' fucking clothes." I pointed to her other knee.

I watched as she took off her clothes. The bitch had all that mouth and was standing in front of me shaking. What a fucking sight, I thought.

"Open yo' legs, ho," I demanded.

I pried her legs open and stuck the butt of the gun in her pussy. I moved it around like I was fucking her. She started to scream as I fucked her harder, not letting up any.

"Fuck you, you stupid bitch. Aargh, oh God, no!" she screamed out in anguish.

The more that ho screamed, the deeper I went in. I wasn't letting up any. This was for all the pain that bitch had put my family and me through. I did not pity her; all I had was hate.

"You see, Shayna, you should've stayed away. Instead, you had to follow me. You had to come here to fuck wit' my child. Bitch, that's the worst mistake you could've made. Never underestimate a mother's love for her child. But you wouldn't fucking know that, 'cause you're not a mother."

"What do you want from me? Is it money? I got plenty of that. Please, I promise, I'll leave you the fuck alone. I got lots of money," she pleaded.

This strong bitch that wreaked havoc in my life suddenly wasn't looking too strong. I knew deep down she was a weak bitch. Blood gushed from her pussy as I took out the gun.

I got closer to her face and looked her dead in the eyes. "No, bitch, I don't want yo' fucking money. What I wanted was fo' you to take yo' old stupid ass away from Alijah and me, but you couldn't respect that he didn't want yo' old, dried-up pussy ass. You had to fuck our lives up."

I then fired three shots into her torso.

"Noooo!" she screamed out. I stood over her and fired the rest of my clip into her body.

I looked at Azir, who was standing in the doorway. "Let's go."

He walked over to her and fired one shot between her eyes. That took the last breath out of her body.

I dialed a number. "Come on in."

"Who's that?"

"Your grandma."

"What? But sh . . . sh . . . she umm—"

"No time to talk 'bout that. Let's get to work and get out of here. Go open the door."

"Oh, I thought you'd never call. Here go the acid." Jeanette emptied three bottles of acid on the body. We watched as this ho's skin melted away. I ain't goin' lie; I almost threw up, but I didn't. I couldn't afford for my DNA to be all over the scene.

"Listen, Azir, you need to gather anything of importance and get outta here. Go to the house and wait 'til I get there," I yelled as loud as I could, with everything in me.

This fucking boy was so hardheaded. I wanted to knock his head off, but I didn't have time, and I needed to get out of here. After he left, Jeanette handed me a bottle of gasoline, and I sprinkled it all over the condo. I made sure the body was unidentifiable. I lit the torch and threw it on her body. Once the fire started, I closed the door and ran downstairs.

I calmly walked to the car, where Jeanette was waiting. I switched places with her. Just in case something jumped off, I was the better driver. I got in and pulled off. I took off my thermal, which smelled like gasoline. I was kind of worried 'bout the neighbors, so I borrowed Jeanette's prepaid phone and dialed 911.

On our way out of the subdivision, I heard sirens coming toward the condo. I drove carefully without bringing any attention to us. I waited until I got out of the area and was back on my side of town to call Azir; he was at my house waiting for us.

Chapter Twenty-One

Sierra Rogers

"Are you ready to go? Your plane leaves at 7:00 a.m. and you have to be there three hours in advance."

"Yeah, I'm set. I still don't want to go; I need to be here for you."

"Sit down." I motioned for Azir to sit on the bed.

"I'm yo' mama. It don't matter where in the world you are; we will always be connected. I lost your daddy, and I damn sure ain't gonna lose you too," I said as the tears flowed down my face.

"Ma, you know what? I love you, woman. Your strength and courage are what gets me through most days. I love you with e'erything in me." He hugged me so tight I could barely breathe.

"Umm, sorry to break up this love session, but my grandbaby, it's time to go," Jeanette said. I could tell she was crying too.

We arrived at the airport just in time for him to check in. I don't know where I found the strength to walk him to check-in. I stood there and watched as my lifeline, my only seed, my heartbeat walked away from my life and into his future. He was headed to England.

"Come on, baby; let's go home. He will always have a part of you in his heart and vice versa. Let's go home."

I collapsed into Jeanette's arms. My heart was broken, and I needed her strength.

"Ma! My baby is gone. He's gone," I cried.

"Baby girl, he not gone. He only went on a long vacation. You didn't have to bury him." She rubbed my back.

"Listen, Ma, I know I never told you, but you're my rock. I don't know where I would be without you right now. I love you."

"Baby girl, I love you too." She took my hand in hers, and we walked out into the brisk air.

"Sierra, cut the television on. Hurry."

My heart jumped; it couldn't be anything good.

"*The Atlanta Police Department gave us this sketch earlier. This person is considered a person of interest in the murder of Dwayne*

McKenzie. *If you recognize this person or have any information about his whereabouts, please contact the APD. Do not approach him, as he is considered dangerous and might be armed,"* the news reporter said. A sketch of a man was posted on the screen, along with a number to call Crime Stoppers.

Jeanette walked into the den and looked at me. No words were needed as we both recognized the picture.

"God, please protect my baby," I whispered.

"I'm going to bed. Long day." I cut off the television and walked upstairs.

Will it ever end, or will this be another saga of heartbreak and hurt? I thought as I dozed off.

The next day I got up out of bed. I wasn't able to sleep all night. My mind was racing. The image of my son's picture plastered across the television screen was still fresh in my mind. I was eagerly waiting on Azir to call me. He promised to call soon as he got a cell phone. I needed to hear his voice, to make sure my child got there safely. "Dear God, please wrap your hand around my baby. Please God," I prayed. I've prayed many times, but this prayer was one that came from the depths of my soul. I knew that I might not see my child ever again, and as much as my heart was breaking behind it, I can't deal with him getting killed or going to prison for life.

This was the risk that I was willing to take. I got up off my knees and sat on the bed. A mother's love is the most powerful, and I would die or kill for my only child. Wherever he is, I pray God protects him. "Alijah, baby, our boy needs us more than ever. If you around, please protect him, 'cause they out to get him the same way they did you."

I felt a tear drop from my eye.

"I love you, Azir."